God's Zoo

ESSENTIAL TRANSLATIONS SERIES 48

**Canada Council
for the Arts**　　**Conseil des Arts
du Canada**

ONTARIO ARTS COUNCIL
CONSEIL DES ARTS DE L'ONTARIO

an Ontario government agency
un organisme du gouvernement de l'Ontario

Canada

Guernica Editions Inc. acknowledges the support
of the Canada Council for the Arts and the Ontario Arts Council.
The Ontario Arts Council is an agency of the Government of Ontario.
We acknowledge the financial support of the Government of Canada
through the National Translation Program for Book Publishing, an initiative
of the Roadmap for Canada's Official Languages 2013-2018:
Education, Immigration, Communities, for our translation activities.
We acknowledge the financial support of the Government of Canada.
Nous reconnaissons l'appui financier du gouvernement du Canada.

God's Zoo

Pablo Urbanyi

Translated from the Spanish by
Natalia Hero

GUERNICA
EDITIONS
TORONTO • BUFFALO • LANCASTER (U.K.)
2020

Original title: *El zoológico de Dios*
Copyright © 2006, Editorial Catálogos S.R.L.
Translation copyright © 2020 Natalia Héroux and Guernica Editions Inc.

Michael Mirolla, editor
David Moratto, cover and interior design
Cover Image: *Girl Kindling a Stove*, Edvard Munch (1883)
Guernica Editions Inc.
287 Templemead Drive, Hamilton (ON), Canada L8W 2W4
2250 Military Road, Tonawanda, N.Y. 14150-6000 U.S.A.
www.guernicaeditions.com

Distributors:
Independent Publishers Group (IPG)
600 North Pulaski Road, Chicago IL 60624
University of Toronto Press Distribution,
5201 Dufferin Street, Toronto (ON), Canada M3H 5T8
Gazelle Book Services, White Cross Mills
High Town, Lancaster LA1 4XS U.K.

First edition.
Printed in Canada.

Legal Deposit—Third Quarter
Library of Congress Catalog Card Number: 2020939316
Library and Archives Canada Cataloguing in Publication
Title: God's zoo / Pablo Urbanyi ; translated from the Spanish by Natalia Héroux.
Other titles: Zoologico de Dios. English
Names: Urbanyi, Pablo, 1939- author. | Héroux, Natalia, translator.
Series: Essential translations series.
Description: Series statement: Essential translations series ; 48 |
Translation of: El zoologico de Dios.
Identifiers: Canadiana (print) 20200257803 | Canadiana (ebook) 20200257862 |
ISBN 9781771835701 (softcover) | ISBN 9781771835718 (EPUB) |
ISBN 9781771835725 (Kindle)
Classification: LCC PS8591.R34 Z6613 2020 | DDC C863/.64—dc23

Although we tell of past things as true, they are drawn out of the memory, not the things themselves, which have already passed, but words constructed from the images of the perceptions which were formed in the mind ...
   —Saint Augustine

[...] and this happened with the dazzling tenderness that is uniquely characteristic of the first experiences of sex.
   —Robert Musil, from *The Man Without Qualities*

1.

He has noticed it more than once: whether or not his past was happy, returning to it is always painful. The happy moments, because they are lost; the difficult ones, because of the pain they revive. Most of the time, he tries to evade them, but, inexorably, they return.

And in this moment, plunged into a dream, they do so with more intensity than ever before. He does not know if he is dreaming, if he is in a hospital because of an accident or some grave illness or if, as his open casket awaits him like a yawn, he finds himself in this infamous final moment before death when one recalls the entirety of one's life. To his surprise, the desire to return bursts in him more powerfully than ever; the desire to be born anew, a desire he knows to be absurd. Absurd, really? He opens his eyes: the ceiling delineates his desire, infinity, eternity. Beyond it, of course, he can picture the sky plagued with stars, and between them, eyes that watched him and that now watch him again, invisible and sorrowful. A starry sky that, day and night, envelops the earth as it travels through space, and he, the star traveller he had always dreamed of being, could dive into the stardust—a haze, perhaps that of a thick wood, densely perfumed with pines—into the mist rising from the moist prairie, from the fresh clovers of the evaporating morning dew. Yes, submerge himself, and hear Judit sing; his first love, who, in the kitchen, would hum a song that went: "A woman is like a wild dove, ever searching for her mate." Yes, this is where he arrives, immersed in the fog, in the darkness of night, but by the light of these fifteen candles (yes, the fifteen, no more no less, that he has left burning), Ipolyság emerges from the haze; the little town of his birth that sheltered and protected him from the war.

He has not yet been reborn, but he is already there. He knows that he will be born and he also knows that, because words obscure the truth, the story of his memories will not be the same and that his old age will compel him to reflect on and interpret the events that comprise it. And so, it is highly likely that, without him realizing it, he may reveal what he wishes to conceal and, for lack of words, conceal what he wishes to reveal.

⤳ 2.

❧——APART FROM THE date that appears on his birth certificate, the date that once was but is no more (although the world in which it saw the light existed already), he does not remember the day he was born nor when he first became aware that he answered to the name Fenix. According to his parents, it was the dawn of a new renaissance for humanity, in which technology, medicine, and other sciences made great strides (the Second World War) when he was conceived in a bed in Czechoslovakia, and, in the same bed, with a flattened head—to the horror of his mother, who took him for an idiot and would treat him as such for the rest of his life, he emerged from her womb, but in Hungary. With time—perhaps because his head rounded out within a few days—he would come to understand with greater clarity this small confusion between nations that seemingly made one same bed into two. He would learn that, due to a lack of textbooks on freedom or any sources of information on any variation of the same theme, children were made in beds and, generally—because of sexual oppression, the lack of free love, and lesbian mothers—with one's wife. And given that medical science had not yet pathologized birth and death, in addition to conceiving and birthing children, one would also die in the same bed at home instead of in a hospital. The change in countries is rather easy to explain: without speaking outright of democracy but (as had been the case since the Enlightenment) starving for liberty, the Hungarians, during his mother's pregnancy, some months before Fenix was born, came to reclaim the territories that had been lost in the First World War. No, he does not remember the day; like any member of humanity, he was born with a blank mind (and, if such a thing exists, a blank soul as well), and without any knowledge of his genetic programming. Nor does he remember his first steps, which must have been hesitant, and which he continues to take without a clear destination. But yes, he hazily remembers: Judit, a small bilingual city, Hungarians and Slovaks living together in harmony and hating each other in secret—as though they had always been there; he has only to close his eyes for them to return, like magic. A city surrounded by a wall that was perhaps built in historical times to keep out Turks or Barbarians or imaginary enemies that could materialize at any moment out in the world unknown beyond its confines. A wall made obsolete by technological advances, but whose shadow safeguarded the city like a second maternal womb. He remembers its narrow cobblestone streets, just wide enough for him to walk hand in hand with Judit; sinister and broken, not designed for cars, barely even for horse-drawn carriages, climbing the Calvary hills and through which, in a child's mind, undoubtedly also trotted D'Artagnan. A tall person could touch both the walls on either side just by stretching out their hands—Fenix dreamed of growing and, one day, accomplishing this feat. There was (or should he say there had been?) a church with two bell towers; the bells could be seen sticking out of one of them, their tolls marking the passage of time hour after hour, spreading mournful news into the ether. There was (or should he say there is still?) a cemetery full of ancient, mouldy tombstones, perhaps centuries-old, ideal for the set of a Dracula movie, as well as more modern ones. Over all of them loomed the branches of weeping willows, nourished by the sap of the dead and the ironwoods, that whistled their laments as they swayed in the wind.

A few blocks beyond the church, a hill. The bottom of it saw the birth of a path; the Path of Sorrows, leading the Easter procession to the Calvary, with believers burdened by a real wooden cross (today they would demand at least minimum wage and stipulate that the cross be made of compressed cardboard or plastic, which imitate wood just as well). At the top, on a small plateau, Christ crucified, his eyelids heavy. On either side of him, the two thieves. The plateau was nestled in a mound that was climbed from the side and on either side of the hill descended rows of vines for local wine. Christ could not see them, but the people asked for his blessing for a fruitful harvest. From there, off to the right, the view bounced between the red rooftops of houses or plunged down into the alleys to arrive at the central square and City Hall, which did not stand out, but it was known that they were there because of the Holy Virgin on the pillar, immortalized in a photograph with Bartók. Below, in front of it, past the vineyards at the bottom of the hill, a winding river lined with trees divided the city into two halves that were merged by an elevated path running through the field and two bridges; the first, over small beaches where children swam in the summer, where the elders fished out of boredom and the poor out of hunger. Under the second bridge, near Fenix's house, a small lake that they skated on in the winter. In the spring, with the thaw, the river overflowed with all the water from the snow on the hills as it accelerated its course. In the forests and the field, waters joined the lake, and often froze over again in the field itself, forming an infinite but dangerous skating rink—dangerous precisely because of its boundlessness, and given its patches of thin ice—where the children, including Fenix, sailed as well as skated. The flood from the thaw—at the cost of the invasion of some houses' basements—made the fields fertile, just like the grounds of little Fenix's palace that could be seen from the Calvary. From there, or any other part of the field, especially in the summer, it was rare not to see the man that had been baptized "The Fool of the Hill" precisely because he was always standing on the hill, motionless as a statue, staring at the horizon, wearing a straw hat, a ragged shirt, and even more ragged pants, leaning on a cane or staff next to his belongings—a bunch of old clothes wrapped in cloth. In the winter he was seen more rarely, and no one knew where he was when he wasn't seen. It was speculated that he hid in some cave in the forest, as though he were a spirit. Some said he was waiting for someone who had abandoned him; others, that he was waiting on a promise (though no one knew what it was) that would never be fulfilled, and that this was the cause of his madness. However, everyone knew when he disappeared for good, and from that day forth they began calling him "The Idiot of the Hill." But, legend or bizarre occurrence, like the apparition of the Virgin, or guilt morphed into a ghost, more than one person had sworn that they had seen him on one of the hills, down to the descendants of those who were present for his name change.

And before bidding farewell to Jesus and descending with a sigh, one could take one final glance at the ruins of the fortress built in the era of Ipolyság's founding, probably the 13th century, or at the alleyways and the wall; these ruins were the only evidence of the city's antiquity and served as proof of the veracity of Marcus Aurelius's *Meditations*. Some, through an eagerness to honour them, said that they had suffered a fate not unlike that of the Parthenon with the Turks. The Russians or Germans had used it as a munitions dump and a violent explosion tore down its walls that had still been standing before the Second World War.

Even further off in the distance: other hills—almost mountains; forests of fragrant pines perspiring sap; steep mountainsides for sleds in winter; wild mushrooms and violets and raspberries in the spring and summer. Unusual forests, to be sure; in addition to those fruits, it was populated by lost souls in mourning, ghosts, and gnomes, awake and alive thanks to the legends that were told, and that still lived on in fairy tales in children's picture books.

The path, which, aided by the bridges that crossed over the lake and river, passed through the street where Fenix's palace stood, leaving to one side the hospital and other houses and streets, forked into two branches: to the left, the Hungarian border; to the right, it ran steeply along the side of the Jewish cemetery and, at the end, broadened and died to give way to the small station at the foot of the hill—a station from whose platform, if one were searching for where the path led, one could see, between the other tracks for the changes or cargo trains, the only pair of tracks that passed through the tunnel and lost itself in the darkness. There were some who claimed, perhaps rather optimistically, that if one focused, a dim light could be seen at the end. The trains that would glide over these rails carried people to other cities, towns, countries, and worlds faraway and legendary. It was said that the tracks led all the way to America, a world full of golden fruit called oranges, fabulous but not yet yearned for.

In addition to a large group of relatives, aunts, uncles, second cousins, grandparents, what else was there or had there been? A band of illiterate gypsies that livened up local parties, birthdays, weddings, and wakes. The blacksmith's, where his grandfather brought his horse; firemen who put out the fires in the fields and pastures; policemen to chase down the thieves and arsonists and throw them in jail; a court that lacked today's tolerance, since there was no need for consumers; and the gallows in one of the City lawns awaiting their next candidate. No one remembered it ever having been used, but, in Fenix's lifetime, it was taken down and it was a real event—not to say a macabre celebration, but ultimately still a celebration. That was a bit of news that, along with other stories, most of which were local, spread through the herald, who with his drum and a strange uniform that gave him a medieval air, made his way through the small city and, stopping on the usual corners, gave a drum roll. The neighbours would run over and once a circle formed, he would unroll a scroll and—horseman of the Apocalypse, in Hungarian or Slovak, or sometimes both, with a thundering voice as though the facts depended on him alone—announce births and deaths, weddings, mayoral activities, prominent and important visits to the city, reminders of parties and, once finished, rolled the paper up to signal the end of the news, said: "I know nothing more, don't press me," and escaped from the crowd that accosted him with questions as though he were the Oracle of Delphi.

In front of the church stretched out a square that, to put it one way, had multiple uses. Every Saturday there was a market there with all the city's provisions; fruits, fresh vegetables, livestock. Two or three times a year, once around Easter, large fairs took place, with cows, bulls, horses, sawn and standing wood. In the middle of the square, a garden with shrubs, benches, flowers and, at the centre, on a large pillar, the Virgin—maybe Mary—wearing a crown of light bulbs that were lit up at night. Forgotten by all (so accustomed were they to her), she tenderly watched over the believers and the harmonious parade of transactions, the just and blessed sales. Every so often a carousel would appear and, very frequently, during the large fairs, hordes of acrobats.

A bakery that sold delicious pies, where the lazy and well-to-do housewives would shop, with outdoor tables. In the summer, especially on Saturdays and Sundays, at a time when the seasonal cycles weren't made obsolete by fridges and freezers, doubly delicious ice cream was enjoyed on the outdoor terraces, where pot-bellied policemen and firemen admired a brass band who barely fit on the small platform, under an awning that shielded them from the sun, elbowing themselves to play more comfortably. Slightly out of tune, they would play military marches and waltzes from the old Austro-Hungarian Empire whose rhythms, like echoes of history hitting the ground, marked with their beats the elders who had disappeared into the sun.

After Sunday mass, visits to the cemetery with aunts and cousins were almost mandatory, for without the custom the obligation would be forgotten and it would become a necessity. There rested Fenix's mother's ancestors and relatives (his father was from other lands and had arrived in Ipolyság like a noble Don Juan, with his ancestors sleeping their perpetual dream in the chapels of their fortresses or the pavilions of their gardens). His mother would introduce him to them as they walked by their graves, saying: "Here lies your grandmother, here your uncle Janos—pride of the family, who died of tuberculosis right when he was about to graduate from medical school, in this other one your great-grandfather, this one is the grave of my twin sister ... and this is where I will rest, next to your father ... well ... I don't know ... I don't much like the idea ... this plot here is reserved for your widowed aunt, they've already buried her husband here ..." And in this way, Fenix could see his growing family, with company guaranteed for all of eternity.

After these appetite-inducing visits came the Sunday lunches, when grace was given to God (rather than the supermarket manager) for the food. These were little parties with all the aunts, uncles, cousins—a family large enough for one not to feel, at least in the memory of the man recalling his story, alone in the world as he is now. Perhaps, if he had the strength (there is nothing to suggest that he doesn't), he would grit his teeth and say: "Yes, alone, in spite of overpopulation." He can recall his widowed grandfather smoking a pipe after lunch, during the afternoon nap—his mother's father, whom she loved very little, and who, since he was young and already married with several children, crossed mountains and valleys, knowing nothing of scientific discoveries and romantic attractions through the spread of aromas from kilometres away, drawn by the subtle and adhesive perfume of the sirens that detained him in other lands, under the guise of buying and selling horses (nothing more than an excuse, according to his mother, since his occupation—always with the same horse, to avoid paying taxes—hid his real business of selling wine to the taverns of the little city and of the small towns that surrounded it). After the Sunday lunches—accompanied by a bottle of his own vintage wine from the vineyard on the hillside of the Calvary, blessed by Jesus up above who, thanks to his pleas for the multiplication or a pact to cultivate wine for mass, occasionally shook his head and gave a sad look out over his property—his grandfather, sitting in an armchair in the living room that they referred to as a lounge, with a voice worn by tobacco and wine, would softly croon; "*Oh, death, deliver the soul with the last breath of love ...*" Under Fenix's gaze, he would doze off with a smile on his face as his pipe went out. There was a slyness in his grey half-open eyes, the muscles of his face relaxed, exuding the satisfaction of having lived. Fenix, now grown, could swear that he was the only happy man he'd ever known. And thus, a decade later, worn by the years, he would die as he sang, with a scandal, but delivering his soul with the last breath of love.

There were other songs, those sung by Judit (whom Fenix has lost forever), that she hummed in the kitchen while she peeled potatoes, or when she looked after him at night, singing him lullabies that went *turururu*. The ones his mother sang, as dusk fell, while she sewed up socks, that he would sing all his life in spite of the advent of the Beatles. He vaguely remembers others that, through the *turururus*, told the stories of soldiers who had been to war, those that returned, those that didn't and those that never would; of adventurers like Robin Hood; of the swallows in the summer that left when winter fell; of storks who built their nests in bell towers; of hills, of land, of landscapes, of wild violets. Oh, so many songs. This, Fenix could easily understand: in those days, his relatives and all the townspeople were dejected beings who knew nothing of comfort. There were only radios with little men speaking inside of them, and there were no tape recorders or cassettes or CDs or stereos or professionals to sing through them. Because of that lack of comfort, they needed to painstakingly express their sorrows, pains, and joys themselves. He also remembers whispers (of fear, perhaps?) about a war, still far away, but that was inevitably approaching.

He remembers a large house that rose up on the first street after the bridge that crossed over the lake where he learned to skate in the winter, hand in hand with Judit. It was almost in the country and was a big house, very big, it really was, or at least to him, a mere child, it seemed like a palace. Behind the house, an orchard, fruit-bearing trees, a vineyard, a vegetable garden, a henhouse, geese, a stable with two or three cows and a pigsty where they would fatten up a pig or two. All tended to by Judit's father, last name Horvath, who lived with his wife, with Judit and her little siblings in a thatched-roof adobe house near the stable.

In those days, in the social class Fenix's parents belonged to, the division of labour between men and women was unclear; rather than by law, it was established by mutual agreement: while Fenix's father went to the city to take care of his business, his mother—for love of power, money or both—was in charge of managing the small barn, overseeing the sale of the milk, butter, cream, homemade cheese, and eggs, as well as counting the money received from Horvath, who, with reverent inclination, called her 'Madam' when he extended his hand with the bills.

Chores were never scarce for anyone and a woman came weekly to clean the entire house and wash and iron clothes. Without the fabulous inventions of the refrigerator and freezer (inventions that not only ruined the simple but double pleasure of eating ice cream in the summer, but also broke with millions of years of natural order), the task of preparing food for the winter—from the slaughter of the pig and the preparation of its by-products, ham and *kolbász* that were hung from the rafters in the attic, to the cooking of sweets and the storage of fruits with methods that today, forgotten, are called secrets—was work that lasted weeks. It was still a rather feudal era and the house, yes, could well have been a palace.

He remembers little of his father's handicrafts factory in the city or, as he insisted on calling it, *artisanal factory*, a name that presented an inherent contradiction, not unlike a political party being called *progressive conservative*. Like a master watching over his cattle, his father went out every morning to supervise twenty or thirty workers. Although he is unable to assign a date to a past so distant, the memory of little Fenix watching his father get ready in front of the mirror to go to the factory or out for other business, when it had ceased existing after the war, is indelible and will never fade. He buttoned up his poplin shirt two by two, his suit of pure English wool made by the best tailors in Budapest, adjusted his tie made of natural silk twenty times, twirled to see how his jacket fell, then one last touch of cologne, light and ethereal, then grabbed his cane with the ivory handle, and, before setting out, examined one shoe to check its shine, then the other, and if everything was in order (and it needed to be with those last few touches: removing any specks of lint off his suit, smoothing out any wrinkles, cleaning off a shadow of dust from his shoe), took one first step out the door, then another, until he disappeared from sight without having noticed the little one, and would leave him there, without saying goodbye with a kiss or a hug, without a little pat on his head, with his hair tediously combed by Judit. How Fenix would have loved for him to mess it up just a little by rubbing his head, or even tug on his ear to punish the little snoop who had the nerve to constantly stare at him, tugs that would at least acknowledge his existence! No, he was never annoyed by his stares: he was attracted to, and distracted himself with, other things, far away. And the boy kept looking for the traces of his father in the mirror, only to see his own funny face instead of the god that had disappeared. In reality, his father went to acquire experience and experiences that down the road, in addition to heroic events and feats that made history, would serve as examples in the teachings he would pass on to his son.

Fenix imagines that his father also worked in the factory, since he must have learned somewhere the trade that he would later continue in the New World to build America. But he imagines something more; he imagines that in the artisanal factory of his native city, his father didn't change very much to work, or rarely did, and limited himself to control and management, another form of work that he would do with a cigarette holder in his mouth on the end of which burned a Corona. In any case, the days were long; a hard-working and responsible man, he would return home late with his clothing a little dishevelled and often enough, his shirt splattered with red paint or some variation of red, proof of his hard work and responsibility. Although she went to church every Sunday, his mother wasn't a believer. So many of her discussions with her husband still echo in Fenix's mind, to this day, always the same ones. It seems that, among the things that he vaguely remembers, in the city, there was a bar, a kind of social club, wherein small tradesmen gathered, who, given that they were the only ones, although few, were the VIP members of the establishment. They gathered to, as peers, in addition to confirm their existence and value, play cards, drink, handle matters that they would consider serious and important and that today would be called market studies or analysis, reaffirm their masculinity with the prostitutes or women of ill repute, to avoid using the direct and unambiguous expression that Fenix's mother tended to use. Yes, he remembers the bar perfectly, it was attached to a hotel, with a revolving door, which, after the war, was associated with two or three dark, shady, at times nauseating episodes, that float in the pond of his subconscious and at times emerge, and he can see the door swallow his father, whom he followed on his mother's orders. Ultimately vulgar police surveillance, although Fenix, his soul conflicted, didn't realize what he was doing in the moment: first, he had to follow his father in the hope that he would pull his ear and mess up his hair, as he had so often hoped in vain, but for that he would need to have been noticed by his father who walked thirty metres ahead of him; but this would have meant betraying his mother, who anxiously waited at home to hear, from Fenix's mouth, the confirmation that yes, her husband had gone to the bar and, as if this weren't enough, Fenix, to get in his mother's good graces, to win her over at any price, would add a fabricated story of an encounter between his father and a woman, probably a prostitute, with whom he would disappear, sucked in by the vacuum of the revolving door. His mother would interrogate him: what did this woman look like, blond, brunette, redhead? How was she dressed, what kind of hat was she wearing, what colour were her shoes? And thousands of other questions that Fenix, dizzied by a feminine vocabulary so rich, to escape, would argue that, having seen them from afar, he couldn't answer precisely. And, after a few seconds of silence, after studying the fierce look in his mother's blue eyes and the way she would wring her hands, in an atmosphere of doubt and ambiguity, Fenix, blushing a little from having betrayed his father and lied to his mother, instead of a prize (a hug, for example), would receive a slap in the face that would make his head spin and mess up his hair, which was one of his wishes. Once his head was back in its place he would hear: "If you say something to your father, I'll kill you." And Fenix would disappear into his room to cry, while, without a father (who, whether in the bar or elsewhere, at that moment, was perhaps engaging in nothing more than the typical black market sales of the postwar period), Captain Vorosoff, who would be his surrogate father for almost a year, would be gone forever. And worse still, so would Judit, his lover, his sister, his mother.

He who remembers his past vividly, more often than not awakens ghosts who, curiously, instead of being fleeting forms and whispers, are like stones, genuine ballasts of the soul capable of paralyzing the mind and sinking it into dark well, as dreadful as if they were in the light of day.

Any traveller, wherever he goes, must stop to rest. So must he who travels to the past. And he who travels toward the new, the unknown, the surprising, the potential change, does so compelled by something well known, familiar, albeit somewhat dishonest, deceptive, and that in the words of Nietzsche, prolongs the suffering of that which we wish to escape: hope.

Travelling to the past can involve something very similar, but the traveller will find more stones than diamonds lost in the meanders of the soul and, even though they provide light, their light will be cold as the eyes of a corpse.

⁓ 3.

HOW OLD WOULD he have been? He doesn't remember exactly. However, more than an exact number of years, he should speak of facts and feats that, although he often sees them from afar as though immersed in fog, he is certain that they existed. A significant portion of his childhood took place in a world in which there weren't as many dangers for a child as in the world of today; as soon as he could walk and talk, he could already go out into the cobblestone streets where there were no blind cars with even blinder drivers. Rather, cows would go by, going to pasture or returning from it, horse-drawn carriages whose drivers would halt or turn swiftly, or the horse would halt on its own or dodge him. Very quickly, his mother's cries, or those of Judit running behind him, would save him from a danger more present in the minds of the two women than in the cobblestone street that the two or three cars of Ipolyság rarely ever drove on. He would go into the small garden, smell the flowers the way he had seen a few adults do and, like them, without knowing why or to what end, would close his eyes, entranced; he would pass by the paths through the vegetable garden, with the tomatoes on one side, lettuce on the other, the carrots over here, cauliflower and cabbage over there. Generally, due to its monotony, without knowing its importance to families and the role it would play during the war, he would stop before the vast area dedicated to growing potatoes, whose sprouts would extend to the edge of the farm, where the flooded river would often reach. Sometimes he would wander to the stable, and inhale the smell of the cows or simply the stable, since the cows and geese, watched over by Judit's little brothers, would graze in the field; other times he would go into the henhouse to run after the chickens and away from the rooster, who would become a dinosaur, chasing him to defend his harem. He would then bolt like lightning through the henhouse door which, with a roar of laughter, Judit's mother or father would close with a comment along the lines of: "You have a long way to go before you're the cock of the walk." Once back in the palace, he would stroll through the different rooms with walls adorned with paintings, with busts mounted on columns of celebrated figures whose voices, although they did have mouths, had been silenced for centuries and never answered the little one. When he played, he would disappear, reappear, and every day he would hide in his favourite place, the kitchen, and there, in a spot he loved even more.

Oh, yes, he was tall; on the tips of his toes, he could open the doors. He would hang from the kitchen door handle and, before pulling it down and entering, with his heart pounding would listen to Judit's *turururu*s. She, in addition to being a cook, girl of many trades, daughter of peasants, her conduct and hygiene under the strict control of Fenix's mother (who would look over Judit's clothes, her ankles, her hands and her fingernails, as with Fenix's before feeding him or tucking him into bed), was his nanny. In the end, perhaps tired of being on the tips of his toes, or because of some internal calling, he would pull the handle and push the door open. Only a little; his eyes would spy through the crack of the half-open door; she would already have heard him, stopped her *turururus* and, from the table where she would peel potatoes or knead dough or clean vegetables, would stare back at him with a mischievous smile, squinting her eyes. Fenix would let out a little chuckle and, as though he were born for this art, he would wait there, watching her. She, perhaps due to her impatience or the boy's innocent sadism, would sometimes threaten him with a wag of her finger, the ingenious boy staring at her broad hips, her breasts beneath the white blouse she always wore, her peasant fortitude that didn't need bloomers to protect herself. She was tall, but she wouldn't have been older than fourteen or fifteen.

How had it all begun? Maybe because of the deficiencies of the past. The time, the days, needed to be filled with life, and little events like their strolls through the cemetery and the Sunday lunches. In those days, there were no professional babysitters to allow mothers and fathers to have their encounters together, or have them with others in strange beds. There was no television either to fill the neurotic void with more emptiness on weekends.

And Judit had to care for Fenix, console him after the vicious beatings and punishments from his mother who, since she couldn't give them to his father, would take them out on him. After the cruellest punishment, kneeling for hours on grains of corn, she would sit him on the kitchen table, rub his knees until the marks disappeared, erase his pain with her tongue and, finally, see Fenix's smile, hear his laughter, thanks to her tickles on the inside of his thighs, and often even further up. Playing with him, listening to him, scolding him, telling him stories, legends of the forest, singing to him, picking him up, shaking him, giving him kisses, loving him.

It may have been in the forest where, on Sunday afternoons or any day of celebration, they would pick wild mushrooms, raspberries, and violets. Or in the fields, where they would search for four-leafed clovers. They would play hide and seek, run, wander around the pasture, and Fenix, sometimes, tired, lying on his back, would look up at the blue, clear sky, with a bird flying through it. The sun would force him to close his eyes or squint and she, leaning on her side, covering him with her breasts, would protect him. On other occasions, on foot, leaning over him, she would watch him and suddenly, lifting her skirt, singing a song and following the rhythm, would jump over him and, instead of a bird, up above, he would see a dark spot that would change places with each of his hops, a black star that forever etched itself into his retinas, and that he saw wherever he looked. Maybe, natural childhood curiosity, he asked: "What's that?" And she, as adults tend to do, would have lied. "A patch of clovers." Is it not normal, then, that lying in the grass at her side, at the edge of the forest, or relaxing with her in the shade of a haystack, or at the edge of the river listening to the soft flow of the water, Fenix, lifting her skirt, sticking his head under it, with her laughing and holding it down with less and less strength, in addition to playing hide and seek, guided by her, would take it upon himself to search for a lucky four-leafed clover there. Had there been anything more sublime in his life than his head resting on that cushion of clovers, while the birds sang or the flow of the river calmed him from the surprises and the emotions which, even though they exhausted him, he always wanted more of? Yes, he would always go back to find the perfume of the wild violets of the forest, of the clovers, of the damp grass.

From the half-open door, he would watch her long brown braids that hung all the way down to her waist, braids that, while she kneaded energetically, would shake from hip to hip, along with her buttocks held up by her thighs, long legs (or they seemed long to the little boy), obscured by her flared peasant skirt that fell all the way down to her ankles. If she took too long, she would stop, fix him with her eyes of the same colour as her hair, but with a golden radiance around her pupils, and would ask him with a slightly broken voice, and which today he knows to have been full of longing:

"What are you doing here? Where is your mother?"

Fenix would push the door, enter and close it behind him.

"She's not here. I want to play hide and seek."

Or maybe:

"I've come to search for a four-leafed clover."

As he approached her, giggles. He wouldn't always do it directly; often, he would turn around, look at the enormous wood-fired stove where a pot was boiling. He would look at the walls, where ladles, spoons, and pot lids were hung, at a painting and an almanac illustrated with the saint of the day. Making smaller and smaller circles around her, he approached.

He would press his little hands and push, and she, bending over slightly, with a meek "No," would push back to stop the little daredevil as she continued kneading, shaking her whole body, or she would start shaking him while she cleaned vegetables. The little hands continued exploring, would go lower, feeling the firmness of her vibrating thighs, and noticing the gentle friction, soft laughter, "I told you, no." The little hand searched for the space between her thighs, a weak resistance, and the thighs would separate and catch it. Reaching the clovers from there was a little difficult, he would pull his hand out and go under the table, his favourite spot, hidden. Once underneath, he would hear, "Fenix, Fenix, I told you, no." On his knees, he would start to lift up the skirt; the sandaled feet would nervously tap the floor, or would move away, laughter, "No," "No," but would soon return to their place. The little hands would continue their search between the legs, at times sheathed by three-quarter-length stockings, white, like a school-girl's. He would try to separate them, so he could see or find something up there, in the heavens, the clover patch. Like magic, the *no no*s and the giggles would quiet and the legs would speak out by putting up a little resistance, and simultan-eously, with soft vibrations, they would cry out. It was beauti-ful, he had to insist. The crisp slip would rustle when, like a monk putting his hood over his head, he would lift it up and penetrate underneath, in the half-light.

He had to get up a little and lift his little hands to be able to hug her thighs; he would press his head against them and, for a few seconds, everything seemed to come to a halt, the roll-ing pin on the dough, Judit's gentle swaying, his little heart, until, the warmth of the thighs that increased their vibrations and shivers, would remind him that there, under that dome, held up by two columns, was the dark cloud that he was search-ing for.

The slip under the skirt continued to rustle while in the darkness, softened by the white light that filtered in through the clothing. Orienting himself and helping himself with his hands, along the front, along the back, always upward, toward the altar, Fenix would place his face between the pillars, as high up as possible, in search of his destination, for that exclamation, that cry, his cheeks between silky pillars, that gently and ten-derly, would part, then squeeze together, throb, tremble, adjust themselves as they shivered; through the skirt he felt her hand, an affectionate, delicate squeeze, on his little head, directing it; he followed, shivered along with her with the first "Ah," weak, higher, higher, "Ah," almost there, answers to his little hands that had approached and were searching for the four-leafed clover; suddenly, always a surprise, maybe the pillars of silk parting, or the cloud of clovers lowering itself, her soul adjusting to his height, her hand collaborating, him finding himself with his face buried in a field of clovers, and Fenix, with his heart pounding, sensing the vibration of her entire body through the silk of her pillars, heard the "Ah"s become more and more frequent, while in the dew of this field, he breathed in the moisture, the scent of the breeze, the caves, the openings of the earth, and the "Ah"s were waves of reincarnation, of rebirth, that went into his little soul, no, she didn't need to tell him anymore, "Your little mouth here," "A long kiss, my little darling Fenix," he already knew, in the four-leafed clover, the taste of the sea, that he didn't know but that he would remember, years later, when he would know it, it was already there; her breath would quicken, her trembling would increase, the wild perfume of the meadow and forest, the depth of the sea, would intensify, Fenix's strange weakness, as well; and the last "Ahhh" was coming, came, long, as though her soul were being delivered, and with which she seemed to collapse, and maybe she leaned on the table, squeezing Fenix's little head; for infinite seconds, moisture and freshness, time and season, stillness of a serene winter snowfall, snowflakes, stars in his eyes; above, in the distance, a vessel toward eternity, a mystery; inside him, strange waves of pleasure, always the same, and yet renewed, increasingly intense.

For the child that he was, heaven on earth, it was the most beautiful place to hide and play with the forbidden fruit. Did he know? The places where it happened, and the way it would unfold, in the field, in the kitchen, when she put him to bed, places decided on by her, probably made him suspect. The astonishment of the change that he provoked, his own change, his strange and foreign pleasure when he listened to the "Ah," made emerge and grow in him not only the desire for repetition, but also, as though this "Ah" were a confirmation of his value, created for him the need to hear it from the mouths of all the women he would go on to love.

In those days, Fenix wasn't very ambitious and staying there to have his little head covered in the bunch of clovers while he hugged Judit's thighs, was enough for him. Sometimes, if he wanted to stay, he would stubbornly stamp his feet, she would indulge him, but sooner or later, rushed by fear, she would make him leave with the promise that soon, it would happen again.

He remembers one day when they were engaged in that struggle, with her trying to make him leave and him, clinging to her hips with his face buried in the clovers: the sound of the door opening, Judit straightening herself out and resuming her work with the rolling pin. Fenix's face had lost this magic pillow and his heels touched the floor again.

He had heard the authoritarian voice of his mother, mistress of the palace, and he had imagined her, occupying the entire door frame because of her stature, with one hand on the handle and the fist of the other at her hip.

"Judit! Have you seen Fenix?"

"No … no Madam … no."

"Where has that little demon gone?"

Speaking of demons, was it he who had inspired her? He would raise his hand up to the clover patch, close it and give it a violent tug. Instead of an "Ah," she let out a loud "Ow."

"What's going on with you, Judit?"

"No … nothing, Ma'am, I hit my finger with … the rolling pin."

"Be careful, I don't feel like eating fingers."
Brammm, the door had shut.

Just like the door, so closes a chapter, the first, in Fenix and
Judit's story. In spite of the infinite times he played hide and
seek, including that Christmas night that he doesn't remember
well, maybe due to having been absorbed in a woman, body
and soul, knowing there would never be another time, there
would never be another time because of that day when ... no,
it's horrible, it's too painful; when during his daydreams her
ghost appears before him, it's as though he is seeing all the
pleasures of life that Judit offered him all over again, only to
arrive again at the final pain. The only consolation that lets
him rest: knowing that she was his true mother and lover without the mortal sin of incest.

Throughout his life, in his body as well as his soul, he has
suffered various types of pain. It has always struck him that
those of the soul, though ethereal, some days more than others,
are practically impossible to erase and that moments of happiness that he had lived couldn't stop them, they never stopped
resurfacing like lashings of the past. Whereas those of the body,
as intense as they had been, ended up disappearing and being
forgotten until remembered again.

4.

❧—THAT CHRISTMAS NIGHT—that unforgettable night that in current terms (with an indulgent smile, of course, it's the memory talking) could be considered the night of Fenix's initiation, through stimuli that he at times recognizes, and at other times doesn't—with the passing of time would become a recurring dream; happy while he sleeps, but painful when he awakens, because it is irretrievable. Always with intense joy, because of the number of times he has dreamed it. At times, in black and white; at other times, lit by the candles and colours of a Christmas tree, he doesn't know anymore if it is only a dream the way that all dreams are, or if it had been a reality more real than reality itself, although he created it with a fortress of words.

However, for that Christmas night to have been possible, some time had to pass in the small city—maybe a year or two, or three. Bah, what does it matter how many, what matters is that he had to grow enough to reach the altar of the dark clover patch; it had now become too easy and, in spite of the variations that the meadow, the forest or the palace itself provided, it ran the risk of becoming as monotonous as a marriage. Although making love was a discovery more ancient than fire and an invention older than the wheel, there were no textbooks about the act, and even if there were in those days, they would only be found in large faraway cities that, for them, were legendary, including Budapest, which was 84 kilometres away. Maybe his father had had one in the library, among the books that were more spoken about than read, but he didn't know how to read yet and, although Judit could, it wouldn't have occurred to her to browse the shelves. She limited herself to reading him stories, fairy tales by Andersen and the brothers Grimm, especially *The Ugly Duckling*, which made him cry and soothed his soul; the already censored versions of *Cinderella*, in the original version of which the stepmother cuts off her toes and heels with a knife to make the shoe fit—something he would only realize years later in a desire to revive his childhood pleasures by rereading the authentic version; other stories, moralizing, that seemed to have been written for intelligent and immoral adults, since he could not understand them; long stories, like the one about the prince who, searching for his eternal love, crossed forests of silver and gold full of danger, for a princess put up for auction by her father, under certain conditions; long stories in which, due to the lack of today's great illustration techniques (which make the text not even seem necessary), he had to strain his mind for the black colour of the trees and their branches to shine like silver and gold. To listen to the variants of love, wouldn't it have been better for Judit to read him the Bible, which contains almost as many beautiful stories, and even more perverse, as the *One Thousand and One Nights*?

Among their favourite stories (and those that provided them both with the most help), were those that Judit would tell by heart: popular legends about the nearby forests, where dwelled gnomes, dwarves that lived underground, ogres in caves that cut children's throats to eat them, even a Dracula in a castle located in the deepest part of the forest where no one could reach; stories that invited a thousand questions and as many answers, that fed their mutual fears and brought urgency to the need to find a four-leafed clover to cling to for salvation.

None of this matters. The passage of time, Fenix's growth, the arrival of the Hungarians to re-conquer the territories lost in the First World War, followed by that of the Germans, who, after a cleansing operation that was a little dirty, disappeared on their way to the front, only to return and leave again running, persecuted by the Russians; the war as a whole would give them opportunities for many variations, from the most beautiful to the most tragic.

The arrival of the Hungarians, who changed the location of the bed where Fenix was conceived and born, represented one of the green lights of the dawn of the war. But the Hungarians (some years later, he would realize) are similar to Latinos. Without any opposition, they tore down the border like the spider-web it turned out to be and strolled in like someone coming home from a walk. At City Hall, they lowered the Czechoslovakian flag and raised the Hungarian. In a solemn act (it couldn't be anything less than solemn) they signed the decree of liberation of this occupied territory. Without worrying about any cleansing operation, like that of Jews and Communists, without wasting any time drinking *mate*, a custom that demands calm, peace and serenity, they continued their march of liberation, slightly zigzagged due to the weight of their equipment, guns and flasks of *pálinka* that, on the topic of cultural comparisons, in alcohol content can be compared to Italian or Argentinian grappa, and went forth to lose themselves on the front lines, which at that moment remained far away, at the ends of the earth. There was a brief lapse of what was once called the "Joyous Peaceful Days of Old," a kind of calm before the storm, while, thanks to a decree left by the Hungarian army, with the collaboration of the Nazi Party, something new appeared in the small city: some people put pretty yellow stars on their chests, like the one that one of the children Fenix used to play with started wearing.

Fenix continued to grow. The game of hide and seek was never lost, but, to their pleasant surprise, without the need for a textbook, and perhaps not even for stories, but rather for "legal" action due to their age difference, little by little they discovered new forms of it. Fenix's mother, considering Judit mature and responsible, without acknowledging that she had been so since the moment she came into the world, made her Fenix's official nanny. In addition to taking care of him, coddling and consoling him, she was in charge of his complete toilette. If today, in the name of hygiene, people bathe every day to the point of damaging their hair and skin, only to repair it afterward with lotions and balms, in these old barbaric times, people bathed once a week at the most, on Saturdays, in order not to offend God's nose on Sundays. Since there was no pollution, there wasn't much to clean either.

On Saturdays, Judit would heat a large pot of water. Since the bathroom (that is, the bathroom with a bath in it) was accessed from the master bedroom, it was prohibited to a child as poorly disciplined as Fenix, who, splashing, could easily have dirtied the room from wall to wall. The hygiene rituals took place in the kitchen sink. With the towel ready, Judit would undress him on a chair, check the temperature of the water and submerge him. First, she would lather him up with a sponge from head to toe, then scrub him, then scrub him again. Although in those days no one spoke of the importance and necessity of sexual hygiene, thankfully, Judit, lovingly, did not neglect it; when her sponge reached Fenix's private parts, she would slow her movements, go around them, put the sponge between his thighs, accompanying the action with soft humming, songs of satisfaction, which, in addition to the caresses, Fenix didn't mind at all. And, one day, suddenly, her humming was interrupted as she stopped, mesmerized by a phenomenon that had never before occurred. Given the almost sacred respect and silence with which she looked upon it, maybe she considered it a miracle, a rebirth. Judit hesitated for a few seconds, maybe a minute; she set aside the sponge to caress it, to play with her fingers, while with a smile and her eyes half-closed, she observed from the corner of her eye the changes and reactions in Fenix's little face—he, as though lost, was also squinting. Thanks to a few variations of back and forth motions, as though she were rubbing a genie's lamp, they discovered an even more significant miracle, a strange one, that hid the skin, and that appeared with an "Ow!" and an "Ah!" emitted by Fenix as he staggered, surprising Judit. Did it scare her, too? What is certain is that she almost forgot to pour water from the jar to rinse the soap off before wrapping him in a towel, lifting him up, and putting him back on the chair. She then knelt in front of it and started drying him carefully as though his body were made of glass, checking at all times whether the miracle was still there. And, for the first time, in addition to the kisses on his little mouth, his neck, his chest, Fenix received them at the site of the miracle, kisses that intensified it. And, also for the first time, after Judit, probably to console him after the "Ow!", opened her mouth to shelter the little miracle, he felt a wetness and warmth he had never experienced before, a shudder that ran through his entire body and almost made him fall from the chair. Fenix understood, suspected, intuited that other destinies awaited them, he and the miracle both. It wouldn't be right to say that on that day, Judit sinned (is love a sin if it doesn't involve deception?); no, without knowing it, she had, very softly, knocked on the doors of desire and awakened him without little Fenix being able to reach this realization in that moment. Maybe on the Christmas night that was fast approaching? Or never, since every time it happened, he would forget it and only a glimmer would remain. Thank God, like a divine sentence or blessing, the desire would emerge again until, one day, it would be nothing more than a vague memory.

By the time she finished dressing him and putting his shoes on so he could go out into a world where magic only existed in legends, the miracle had vanished. But he would continue his discovery during an imitation of what was once called "The Joyous Peaceful Days of Old," two or three years before the war, through a window, arrived with thunder and lightning.

"Peaceful Days?" The herald and his drum had disappeared. They were replaced by the radio, which, instead of just one, had multiple people inside (little talking men, to Fenix). Thanks to a knob, a technological marvel, you could make them announce the news at whatever volume you wanted, even making them shut up if they said something inconvenient or dangerous that would be better not to know about—or that you could be punished for knowing. His parents spent all their time with their ears glued to it, moving the needle like diviners searching for a treasure, and only heard voices in unknown languages, that made it a tiny tower of Babel. For some reason (and despite the fact that he spoke it, because it was a distinguished language and a kind of *lingua franca* of European culture), his father wasn't interested in the German from Germany, nor the Russian from Russia that he and Fenix understood mainly because they had learned Slovak—his father, for business reasons; and Fenix, from playing in the streets of a bilingual city. What were they looking for? Probably, from other, more truthful sources, announced in some of the languages they understood, news of triumph, glory, and the return of "The Joyous Peaceful Days of Old," like the return to the Lost Paradise or to others that never existed, and if they did exist, only in a state of loss. Invariably, they would turn off the radio, shaking their heads with worry. Although there was no drummer, sometimes so loaded with *pálinka* that his reading was almost incomprehensible, on the radio, a precise instrument, the news from the little men didn't seem any better or more trustworthy than those of the herald: the threat loomed over the "Peaceful Days." Or, between a yes on one side, a no on the other, in different languages, the news was so contradictory that it confused minds that were already confused by virtue of their existence. Whether because the Hungarians weren't doing their duty at the front, no more than they had done during their passage through the city, or because there was some truth to the lying news from both sides, there occurred another important event: the arrival of the good Germans to crush and annihilate the bad Russians for good.

As soon as the Germans appeared on the horizon, as though they were pushing air more solid than a stone block, Fenix's parents, almost without him noticing, were displaced, or, by magic, evaporated in that same air. When Fenix noticed the spaces that their shapes had left, he asked his grandfather, who paced around the palace more and more, where they had gone. His grandfather would take his pipe out of his mouth and grunt impatiently: "They were swallowed by the earth."

Rumour had it that Hitler was in possession of a secret weapon that would ensure his ultimate victory in the war—although, they said, it wasn't quite ready and still needed a few finishing touches. However, the German army, the best in the world, was invincible, so there was nothing to worry about. Under the watch of half the city, including Fenix, and Judit who held his hand, they entered little Ipolyság, elegant, clean and disciplined, triumphant, serious as death and joyfully singing something like *Deutschland, Deutschland Über Alles*. Bearing the swastika as their trademark, they brought tanks, half-tracks, ambulances, field kitchens, trucks, cars, motorcycles, and enormous hounds, worthy of successful feminists, which, when Fenix would pet them, under the smile of the soldiers that held them on chains, showed their teeth almost the same way that today's police or special forces do, in a world so ragingly free and democratic. They needed to stay for some time. They lined up their vehicles along the entirety of the street where Fenix's palace stood, along with the base of what might have been the high command, which Fenix would wander between without much consciousness of what it all meant. Apart from the hounds, what drew his attention was all the raising of hands with the palm facing downward, and all the tapping of heels echoing, which slowed the fulfillment of orders. Spying through the open doors of some of the bases that he would access by climbing a few steps, he would see maps on the walls, and there they were: on their feet, gathered around a table, leaning over it, listening to the booming voice of one of them and attentively following his index finger as it travelled across the surface and that, every now and then, would tap on certain spots, taps that, as though their heads were being pulled by a string, they would all nod along with. Recalling this sight, years later, Fenix would realize that it was about the study of tactics and the planned (not to say imaginary) preparations for the bombings and attacks to destroy the bad Russians. And he would remember something else; its insignificance to him as a child when, after some time spent circulating between them and entering the quarters as though he were invisible, even the ones that were used as dormitories, from which, out of discomfort (not frequently, but the women that he sometimes discovered in the beds, sleeping or watching him with a teasing smile, and that were familiar to him due to his having seen them in the street, now that he thinks of it, were the same ones that entertained the local bourgeois at the bar) and a little fear (remembering his mother's fits of rage and insults toward these women), he would run away from. Once, however, he stayed to watch an official who, in front of a mirror on the wall, was fixing his cap, taking an infinite amount of time to arrive at a perfection non-existent in theory but real in practice when, hat and head together as a unit, he nodded in the mirror and left without having even looked at little Fenix, who remembered the habits of his father, who was still missing and whom he missed. Confronted with these signs of inexistence, without owning property but with bourgeois pride, he would sniffle and dry his eyes with his sleeve, consoling himself by thinking of how his father's mirror was much, much bigger; he could fit in it from his silk tie all the way down to his shoes, as opposed to the official, who needed to constantly bob up and down, barely fitting in his as a hat-and-head entity.

Was it in the middle of summer or at the end of it? It doesn't matter, not even in his memory. Due to the troops' movements, the military exercises of the Germans, secret things, the meadow, and the forest remained forbidden for all citizens, even Nazi collaborators. It wouldn't have been an inconvenience; with the mysterious disappearance of his mother and father, the palace would have been practically empty and at Fenix and Judit's complete disposal so they could play their games without needing to hide (and, upon losing the taste of the forbidden, the secret, the delicious complicity, they would quickly have grown tired of them), if his grandfather hadn't moved in with them, armed with two demijohns full of wine, some clothing, a carriage that he parked behind the palace, and a horse that he entrusted Judit's father with the task of putting in the stable. The mischievousness had disappeared from his grandfather's eyes and as though he had lost control of his pipe, it smoked irregularly; or, due to his puffs, it came out as dense columns of smoke, or nothing came out at all, no matter how furiously he pulled. As time went by, Fenix's questions, anxious and insistent, returned: Where is Mother? Where is Father? Judit would answer that she didn't know but that they would be back soon. His grandfather, caressing him clumsily due to lack of practice, would say the exact same thing.

Because the Germans set up headquarters on the same street as Fenix's palace, it was impossible not to notice them. One day, as she was leaning over the kitchen table, through the window, in the courtyard, Judit saw a dashing officer with beautiful piercing blue eyes, wearing a freshly ironed uniform and boots shiny enough that you could fix your hair or hat in the reflection, who, while nodding, studied the entire palace, from the ceiling to the windows, walls, and staircases. He would walk with steps carefully calculated, measured and rehearsed in a school for high-ranking officers. They were rhythmic steps that could very well have accelerated according to the circumstances or even come to an abrupt potential halt, ready for an immediate departure. And he did. The two soldiers who were escorting him with machine guns hanging from their shoulders and who were probably following his steps, also halted and, with a gentle tug on the chain, stopped the dog that one of them was holding. By the time the blue eyes noticed Judit on the other side of the window, Fenix had climbed onto the table and on his knees, with his arm hanging from Judit's neck, also caught the attention of the blue eyes, which nodded and turned along with the officer's head to fix one of the soldiers and give him an order. A click of the heels and the soldier, with a spring in his step, climbed the stairs that led to the palace's front door, a double-leaf door that gave way to a spacious veranda sheltered by a roof light, full of winter plants, and from which some of the bedrooms and hallways could be accessed. The soldier didn't bother looking for a doorbell or a knocker; with his fist, he hit the doorframe with such vigour that his knocks were not only heard by the half-deaf grandfather, but were loud enough to wake the dead. His grandfather answered with his unlit pipe; none of the languages he knew (not Hungarian, nor Slovak, nor International Sign Language) were enough for them to understand each other. The officer went up; as energetically as the German was speaking, the grandfather couldn't understand the language of great poets, philosophers, metaphysicians and the world's most powerful army. In cases of war and domination, it wouldn't make much sense to speak of courtesy. However, since it costs nothing to be kind, the official was; with his hand on the grip of his Luger pistol, he gently pushed his grandfather aside, passed by Judit and Fenix (who noticed the fear in Judit's hand that was holding his), and with the same kind of steps as in the courtyard, he patrolled the long and wide veranda, stopping before each plant and studying it like an expert; more than once he shook his head. Before opening each door, he would point with his index finger and look at the grandfather, who would shake his head no. Probably now convinced that no one else lived in the house, he ended up choosing the first bedroom from the entrance. It was, if Fenix is remembering correctly, a large room, with a Russian ceramic wood-burning stove, smaller than the one in the living room; a bedroom which, in addition to being used for visitors, of whom the officer was the first Fenix could remember, was meant to enlarge the living room with a double leaf sliding door, which the German, maybe in order to see the enemy coming from afar, would henceforth leave half-open. Or maybe not; since the door frame was a kind of arch, as a symbol of triumph, he used it to enter and leave instead of those that gave way to the veranda.

That same day he settled in and the next morning, he had the biggest plant in the veranda removed, the one with thousands of little leaves. Under the curious gaze of Fenix, after pulling off all the leaves that were dried and yellowed, with the patience and love that not even a delicate embroiderer would have, with a little wet cloth, one by one, he cleaned each leaf of the tree, pulled out the weeds and removed the soil from the barrel that served as a pot, watered it, the tree reflected in his blue eyes, with he used to stare at it for a while with a satisfied smile, maybe even affectionate, and stroked the leaves as though he were petting his favourite dog or cat.

And, without having noticed Fenix's existence, he gave the order for them to take it back to the veranda.

5.

THE FUTURE, FOR a child, with a mix of narcissistic impatience and an inability to tolerate frustration, is or should be something immediate. Thus, although Fenix would learn this much later on, and although they would tell him that his parents would be back soon, this didn't stop him from asking every day. It was more likely that his grandfather knew where they had gone and why, but Judit, whose love seemed to have gone cold, did not. However, as far as love was concerned, it was quite the contrary; Judit never took her eyes off him and her embraces were stronger than ever, but, against her will, they carried with them a certain amount of fear that manifested in light trembling; fear and trembling that, without her realizing it, were speaking to Fenix. Aside from the disappearance of his parents, a disruption that his grandfather couldn't make up for entirely, through the thousand rumours that were circulating, Fenix would learn something, or worse, would only suspect it and, without having any certainty nor the ability to verbalize it, it would turn into the worst kind of fear, the fear of the unknown, which penetrated his tender soul the way viruses enter the body.

Not always, but in general, sooner or later, when it comes to mystery, secrecy and human intentions, and not mysteries like the existence of God or the origin of the universe, the truth, or what is believed or assumed to be true after hearing it repeated enough, always ends up revealing itself. And that is what happened with the task that the Hungarians didn't complete, or rather that they considered complete as they swept it under the rug. The Germans inevitably considered it to be dirty work. As a result, they launched into a cleansing operation that could be considered an ancestor of the present-day pathological obsession with hygiene and purity. Obviously the soul did not enter into the operation, since the hunted prey that the Germans considered dirt to be swept under the rug didn't appear to have any either. If by chance one of these prey had managed to have one, it wasn't very visible, or rather was ethereal, and through the chimneys, it would ascend to the highest heights without the members of humanity hearing a cry of pain.

Fenix doesn't know if in those days the infamous concept stating that although life may be lacking, colour livens it, existed. It must not be a coincidence that today the world is so tacky, full of bright colours. How, when and why the yellow stars that shone twinkling on the dark suits of those guarded by the German soldiers appeared (there was talk of volunteers who had prepared lists with addresses and family names that spoke for themselves), Fenix would only know and understand a decade later. With Judit holding, or rather gripping, his hand, he would watch the gallant march of the soldiers, who if it weren't for their hounds, would have looked like guardians of honour or of the corps that accompanied the Jews to the station to load them into wagons that would carry them off to who knows where and that, for the majority, souls evaporated through chimneys, would be a one-way trip.

However, at that moment it didn't seem like it. Or rather, because of the minimal, sometimes luxury baggage they carried, one might even think they were taking a plane to America, the one and only America, also known as North America or the United States. But, no. There was something that didn't add up. The march, from a human point of view, was silent: no one spoke. And silence has no memory if it isn't populated with sounds. A strange dragging of feet that could have been tired just as it could, involuntarily, have been from dread, a reluctance to go where they were being led. Other sounds? Cries of pain from someone, tired or old, who wasn't marching forward to the harmonious rhythm imposed by the soldiers. Or no, the cry of someone undisciplined that had stepped out of line, that not only received a blow with the butt of a rifle, but also a bite from a hound trained to care for the Lord's flock.

Yes, Fenix remembers this populated silence, but, would he remember his own cry of surprise, a "Hey!" that was lost among the others? Judit's hand squeezed harder to hold him back or stop him running to find the best friend he had in those days and that, in the middle of the file, a little lost, marched, pushed along by his brothers and sisters. Judit did something more: with her other hand she covered Fenix's mouth when he was about to call his name to get his attention and wave his hand to say goodbye to him until his return, which would never come.

Fenix became furious. The son of the royal family of the palace, the prince, being held back from running and having his mouth covered! And he turned against Judit to start kicking her, punching her or whatever else he could manage. And he had stopped cold.

Yes, it was possible, almost certain that Judit knew or, worse, feared it was even worse than she told him; her eyes full of tears served as evidence.

His heart softened; he stopped at that moment so as not to make the person he cared about most suffer. Today he suspects that she saved his life: if he had gone to join the flock of sheep, the wolfhounds or Lassie dogs like in the movies wouldn't have let him leave; or if he had cried out from the path, some soldier might have thought he was out of place. When they got home, he asked Judit:

"Where is David going?"

Judit sighed.

"I think ... on vacation. Yes, on vacation."

"On vacation? With all those people? And the soldiers?"

"Right ... it's a lot of people ... And the soldiers ... well, they're looking after them ..."

There were no more questions. If she had gone on, she would have had to confess that she didn't know either where they were being taken. She knew, yes, or rather she could guess, that whatever the reason, the soldiers' presence wasn't a good sign.

Once the cleansing operation was complete (whether or not they washed their hands, Fenix had no idea), the Germans started their engines, lined up the cars and tanks, and, under the watch of fewer citizens than before, elegant, clean-shaven, with washed faces, with the same discipline that they entered with, though a little less austere, perhaps satisfied with the task they'd completed, singing *Deutschland, Deutschland Über Alles* with enthusiasm, they re-embarked on their triumphant march toward the front.

The last days of summer and first days of autumn had gone by. The ritual of cleaning the leaves that Fenix had observed two or three times had lasted up until then. The officer, before descending the palace steps and climbing into the car that awaited him, with profound sadness in his eyes (that twinkling, was it from tears?), left the plant behind with some instructions for his grandfather who, nodding, understood absolutely nothing. Maybe they were recommendations for whoever was going to look after his beloved, whom he said goodbye to with a few caresses and soft kisses on its leaves.

In the history of humanity, the romantic relationship of the officer came to a close with an energetic spit onto the plant from the grandfather.

6.

&——**THE ARRIVAL AND** departure of the Germans was celebrated by many. Like in democracies with the For and the Against, people had their respective reasons. Those who had collaborated with them and stolen the Jews remained as leaders in the city; a little servile, but leaders all the same. The patriots, on the other hand, were happy to see the mob leave and prayed to God that they would meet their end at the front. What was, justly or not, called "The Joyous Peaceful Days of Old" returned and, for a brief period, acquired meaning once more. Fenix's mother reappeared; his questions about her absence were futile. He knew that insisting would be like provoking the ire of the gods and bring about thunderclaps that would resound like the echo of a slap in the face. For her, for the good of everyone, she said, instead of explaining where she was, it was more import- ant to regain control of the palace, put the disorder back in order and restart what had stopped. Did those Germans steal anything, that bunch of ...? No, including the officer that lived here, he was a gentleman. If he stole anything it was dust, be- cause in the bedroom everything shone as though brand new. Holding Judit's father to account was a more complicated matter. Horvath was a peasant and, although "those kinds of people" were associated with vulgarity and ignorance, as defined by the lords, Fenix's mother knew perfectly well that many of them are clever, even liars, and that one must be careful with them, like dealing with a fox. Fenix's mother suffered genuine existential torture thinking of how many of the eggs that the chickens, ducks, and geese were laying daily were being eaten or renegotiated behind her back by the cunning Horvath, who wouldn't stop insisting: "But Ma'am, neither the chickens nor the ducks, and especially not the geese, lay their eggs every day." Fenix's father would mock her, suggesting that she sit in front of the animals' asses to count them herself and figure out the average since, from what he had heard from other sources, they didn't all lay an egg every day. After two or three months of absence while the Germans had been here, the Mistress asked Judit to go fetch Horvath and, to avoid him dirtying one of the covers of the chairs in the living room, the first meeting between her and the peasant, who entered with his hat in his hand, took place in the palace kitchen and was a genuine clash of the titans. The first shot fired by the Mistress was:

"How many eggs in total did you collect and sell during my absence?"

As though he got his ideas from there, as opposed to his head, he made his hat spin in his hands as he spoke.

"No idea, Ma'am, you know that I don't keep track, if I did, I don't know if I'd be able to count that high a quantity but, in addition to supplying the palace, don't forget that your son and father were here, plus some for us every week, and especially because of the thefts of chickens and ducks and the trouble the Germans would cause the poor little animals that were left, God's creatures, because we all are, there weren't many."

"The Germans stole? It was my understanding that the Germans paid for their provisions."

A spin of the hat.

"Well, to me, never. They didn't consider me important. Maybe if you, Ma'am, had been here. Obviously they didn't do it visibly. Imagine. If I had ..."

"And the milk? How many litres?"

"Litres? Well, I have no idea. But, with the racket the Germans were making and how it upset the poor little cows, they didn't manage to produce the amount that they usually would. Believe me, it was hard, really, really hard!"

"The Germans again? What do the Germans have to do with the cows?"

Without knowing it, and without knowing its history, the peasant Horvath laid out the basics of the notion of stress and its fatal consequences. His eyes filled with tears and with a pained voice, while his hat spun in his hand more quickly than ever, he explained:

"Yes, Ma'am, not only are chickens and ducks God's creatures, but so are cows. And they're more sensitive because they're bigger. It broke my heart when, early in the morning, my children brought them back in, because the Germans wouldn't let them go out to pasture. Without that freedom, and the fresh grass that they would eat in the field, they would come back looking sad, with their heads down. Once back in the stable, I needed to feed them hay, which they ate reluctantly. And you must know, it's just not the same, hay that ..."

"Enough! Did you make cheese?"

The hat became still. Probably, for the first time in her life, from a peasant or anyone else, his mother received a look that made her feel like a fool, her inflated self-esteem saving her from feeling stupid.

"No milk, no cheese, ma'am. Barely enough to feed the boy, the grandfather, and the tiniest bit left over for us."

"Aha, and the cream? Did you make butter?"

The Mistress never knew why the hat's movements, this time oscillating back and forth, reminded her of a smile.

"But, Ma'am, the milk was so thin you almost couldn't skim it."

"Enough, please! Let's move onto something else. I see the fruit trees are bare."

"I don't understand you, Ma'am. You know it better than I do. The harvest season is over and we're almost in the middle of winter."

"Sure, but where is the fruit?"

"The Germans, Ma'am, the Germans. The apples that I was able to save are in the attic."

And so it went, until they both ended up spinning like the hat in a whirlwind of frustration and rage in which words became futile and lost their meaning.

Fenix's mother, as a lifeline, ended up asking for the money that Horvath had raised from the sales and, without counting it, to avoid worsening and prolonging the feeling of defeat, put it in her pocket, stood up and, standing tall, taller than ever, as though she were saying *Vade retro Satanas*, showed him the door.

Once the peasant Horvath had closed it behind him, the hat started spinning again around his index finger.

One could rightfully ask which of the two was left queasier, between Horvath who seemed to have had some *pálinka* or the Mistress who would have gotten drunk off cognac or some other fine liquor.

And the "Peaceful Days" continued. The grandfather stayed with them. Every now and then, he would take a ride around the city to refill his demijohns in his home winery, at the foot of the Calvary and stock up on tobacco, ever scarcer; for that, apart from the tobacco shops , glass upon glass of *pálinka*, or glass upon glass of wine, he would frequent the taverns whose owners were more sensitive to human weaknesses and to the black market. There, in addition to tobacco, as though he were listening to the little radio men, the grandfather would gather news that circulated through word of mouth and that, although it is said that children and drunks speak the truth, were not always trustworthy. His father had not returned. If it was because of his questions, or a strange association of the mind that travelled from the past to the present or from the present to the past, or because of what he would come to understand over time, he knew, and knows today, that his father had disappeared in order not to complicate the cleansing operation for the Germans and his lack of enthusiasm for ending up six feet under. As a member of the Communist Party, he fought for the well-being of the people, whom he referred to as "the shapeless masses" and that he had despised all his life; now, in the "Joyous Peaceful Days of Old," somewhere, with optimism, he waged guerrilla war against the invincible army.

Apart from an approximate amount of time measured based on other events, it is absolutely impossible for Fenix to remember exact dates. Since the time of his discovery of the enchanted clover patch, his reactions during his Saturday baths, as well as those that Judit contributed to some nights during which, before going to bed, she would read him stories while, instead of the bath sponge, her fingers, like the wands of a fairy, would create the miracle that would make him say "Ow," and that she, to alleviate the pain, after looking at him with a smile, a cunning reproach in her eyes, would moisten so that his soul would breathe out an 'Ah' of sweet release, from that time until the

Christmas night that he still dreams of in colour, passed two or three years. He could already open doors without standing on the tips of his toes and during the games of hide and seek with Judit, she didn't need to adjust to his height, except for, by spreading a little, taking care so as not to hit his head on the table. His final 'Ah' wouldn't only produce waves of pleasure anymore, but rather a strange and infinitely pleasant throbbing in the miracle that always ended in a shudder. He also remembers that he had received his first long pants as a diploma recognizing his growth, or because of the winter that was opening its doors. He prefers "being sure" of the former. There was no shortage of other memories: he would already have gone to school, but because of the war, it was impossible and even more so because of what the little radio men were saying; the front of what was called the Second World War, had stopped its advance, had reversed its direction, and had filled itself with threats, punishment for some, and began approaching the residents of the little city.

It had already been a while since the First World War ended. It had barely brushed by Ipolyság. Of those who had participated in it, a few now senile geezers, many couldn't tell their tales, there was little left in their memory: they would only blabber, talking about lice, and hunger, and of their own feats that nobody understood anymore or the younger ones, impatient, didn't want to understand or appreciate. In the face of memories so hazy, the lack of Hollywood movies and their simulation techniques, the sound that war made was unknown, its music, its noise, the roar, the blood, everything that war, in this case the front, brought with it. Without this historical memory, the details of the horror were unknown and the imagination, or the legends that emerged from who knows where, multiplied and intensified them. The Germans were already known: they were only doing their job and they were good, extremely clean, real gentlemen. But, from what they heard, the Russians killed, raped without discrimination, robbed, tortured, looted and God knows what else. The fear bordered on terror, grew, and all the preventative measures seemed useless. For the first time in her life, maybe the only time, his mother neglected her management duties of the palace and, like a commander in chief, authority that gave her her husband's nobility (or supposed nobility) by osmosis, to which was added the wealth she had compared to her poor parents, gathered with her sisters (half-sisters, this too he would only realize later) to arrange the moving of various families to the basement of some of the neighbourhood houses or the palace's, which was the biggest.

The first real concrete news was delivered by the grandfather. It was the reappearance of the first trucks of the Germans who, as an ancestor to the concept of recycling, dedicated themselves to the recollection of everything that was a tool that, according to the laws of the market, supply and demand, in that situation of the stock market of war, was more valuable than gold. The machines and motors of his father's artisanal factory turned out to be a goldmine that they left exhausted. The trucks left their tracks in the snow and disappeared toward their cherished homeland.

And the wait for the arrival of the front continued.

7.

&—IN HUNGARIAN CULTURE, although the "Epiphany" is known as the day when Christmas trees are taken down, the Three Kings don't come on their camels to hand out the gifts that the children asked for. This is a task (including the tree with its decorations and lights) for the baby Jesus on Christmas Eve, which is more realistic than the gift-giving of the Kings (or of Santa Claus) given that Jesus, son of God and God Himself, although still a baby, is infinitely more powerful and capable of fulfilling all wishes, as outlandish as they may be. On the Eve of the Christmas that Fenix remembers with such intensity, in the end, under the tree, Judit had assured him, he would find what he had wished for: an electric train that he had seen making circles in the window of a toy store, or maybe he had seen one of his friends' fathers operating one, he doesn't remember exactly. When he asked for it, it was explained to him that it was still very dangerous for him, since he was just a child—not because of the train itself, but because he wasn't fully aware of the dangers of electricity. It seemed as though these explanations were Jesus's answer to Fenix's wish, which he received through Judit since his mother and father limited themselves to a quick and cold "You're still too young." Thank God, Jesus (they are one and the same) promised that one day he would receive it.

Time isn't interested in the dates that mark human lives. But since they do mark them, sooner or later, and even more so when it comes to the way they unfold in the past, they arrive, inexorably, at the perfect time.

Thus, since there is no deadline that doesn't arrive nor debt that goes unpaid, especially if Jesus is involved, the Christmas night on which the baby Jesus fulfilled his promise and it was the same one that, dreamed or not, became unforgettable, as much for its happiness as for its pain: longing, and the infinite desire of repeating the impossible.

On that Christmas night, in the palace's living room, with a huge Russian ceramic furnace and a grand piano with black varnish for the private and intimate concerts that any palace could hold (although not a single one was), for the first time in his life, like the revelation of a secret, Fenix helped with the decoration of the pine tree, twice his height, and whose star was placed by Judit, who stood on a chair. This was how he realized that not everything was brought by Jesus (although there wasn't talk yet of overpopulation, there were millions of children) and that he needed help. In a moment of carelessness by Fenix, aided by Judit, Jesus quickly fulfilled his promise, announcing it with the sound of chiming bells. Fenix ran; in addition to the smell of pine, the forest breeze, his nose was invaded by the smell of wax from the candles that his grandfather had just lit. His mother entered, and the four of them together, obediently following the ritual whose origin was unknown, knelt in front of the tree and thanked God the Father and Jesus the Son for the gifts under the tree, among which stood out a large box; Fenix, distracted during the prayers, with the certainty this was "it," didn't take his eyes off of it. It wasn't a very long prayer, no one's knees hurt, no one gave thanks to the Holy Two-for-One for the war, the front that was approaching and with it, inevitably, the bombs, which would fall like a punishment for their sins, for which reason they considered it futile to beg for forgiveness. After grace, they limited themselves to reminding God that they were alive and that they remained in that state as a prize for the sins they didn't commit, for which they were grateful to Him.

Once the brief ceremony had ended, since there would be no Christmas Eve dinner, the mother ordered Judit to give Fenix something to eat, put him in his pyjamas and put him to bed early, since not even God knew what might happen the next day.

His mother, wrapped in an astrakhan coat bought in Budapest, and his grandfather, bundled up in a long lambskin coat on the outside and a glass of wine on the inside, went out into the cold to meet up with the relatives. They needed to organize the layout of the basement to protect themselves from the bombs and grenades, prepare the provisions for who knows how long, and move down there before the front arrived.

Fenix rushed over to the box. Although in those days neither the tree nor the world was made of plastic and there wasn't as much danger as today that it would catch fire, Judit went to put out the candles with her fingers, passing them between her lips to wet them with saliva. Afterward, while Fenix busied himself with the electric train box, from which he removed wagons and rails, and searched for the locomotive without which nothing would move, Judit loaded the Russian ceramic stove with logs and left its door open. She sat down, joined her legs together with her arms, rested her jaw on her knees and, pensive, stared at the fire; the flames had begun to grow and were devouring the logs. Every now and then, drawn by an exclamation, by a noise, by her duty, she would lift her head and turn to look at Fenix who now, after having laid out all the parts, with ingenuity, without needing the instruction manual, like an educational puzzle, began preparing the tracks.

Outside, a world of snow; inside, an open fire crackling. Fenix was busy doing wonders with what was available; a locomotive with two wagons for passengers, a cargo wagon, a tank to transport water, a long, curved pulp board tunnel, a railroad crossing sign, an elevated station with a platform and a transformer with a key through which passed a cable from the wall to the platform, under the station waiting room. The rails in place, with a closed curve through which the train would turn around before resuming its path. He had barely put the locomotive on the rails to undertake a trip to the ends of the earth when he heard a hoarse choked up voice that, if he hadn't seen Judit standing next to him, he would have thought belonged to someone else.

"Come, Fenix, you need to eat dinner and put your pyjamas on."

Where we learn or copy certain gestures from, we don't often know. Fenix put down a passenger wagon on the tracks, stood up—if not at her height, his head at least reached above Judit's waistline—and with his hands on his hips, just like his mother, who, in fact, he didn't love, fervently exclaimed:

"No. Later. I'm playing."

At any other moment, Judit would have lifted him up and, with the help of a few jokes, caresses, or soft nibbles or tickles, would have turned his refusal into resignation; but was it her red eyes, her sad and languid smile, which Fenix saw but did not have those words to describe them as such, that defeated him? This remains uncertain; like the time Judit covered his mouth so he wouldn't scream and he wanted to attack her, he felt the slackness which, he didn't know, was that of submission, almost a surrender. Without a word, he held out his hand to Judit, who led him to the kitchen. Since no one had fed it for quite some time, one of the occupations that people spent their lives doing in ancient times, the wood-fired stove had gone out and would need to be lit again.

"Brrr, it's cold in here," Judit said, shivering.

From the dough prepared for the Christmas festivities on the table, she cut pieces of a poppyseed, nut, and apple roll; she loaded up a plate and gave it to Fenix.

"Here. Take this over to the tree, carefully, and wait for me there."

Fenix complied without a word, since the train awaited him there.

Judit didn't run, but her steps were quick and furtive. She fetched a pair of pyjamas from Fenix's bedroom and when she returned, with a glass in her hand, she went into the pantry that was always colder than the kitchen itself. She took out a pitcher of milk and filled the glass. In half a minute, with her legs crossed, she was seated in front of Fenix, near the fire.

If there are gestures that, through being habitual, seem inexplicably natural to us, those that are unusual are even more difficult to explain. Fenix and Judit were eating and sharing the glass of milk in a way they never had before: in a solemn, church-like silence, as though they were drinking from a chalice; a silence broken only by the crackling sound of the logs in the fireplace—which, as though a freezing cold draft may come in through the doors and windows, Judit had loaded again. She was worried about something, there was no doubt about it. And Fenix, every now and then, fearing that the wagons and cargo may somehow get away from it, glanced at the locomotive.

The glass of milk was emptied, Fenix's hunger was satisfied, and he was already attaching the wagons to the locomotive. Once the last one was hitched, he turned the key of the transformer and, slowly, the train was put into motion, pulling the wagons behind it. It completed one turn, then another, and another. Suddenly, he yawned without covering his mouth. Turning the key, through trial and error, he managed to park the train right in the station; the Germans had arrived with the people wearing the bright yellow stars, including his friend, always watched over by the Lassie dogs, who were in so many moving films, genuine heroines that did more good for humanity (at least when it comes to distractions) than human beings themselves. With his face glued to the window, David looked at him with a smile, happy to be going on vacation; Fenix had given him a hug on the platform, waiting for the train to leave. He turned the key, the train slowly pulled out of the station and David was waving him goodbye, goodbye, and Fenix too; the train went off into the distance, into the dark tunnel and, without him knowing it at that moment, for a second time, he lost his friend forever.

To fight boredom, everything is easy, so easy that it isn't worth talking about; it's enough to say that the world, the earth, the cities, the streets, the houses, are no more than a vertigo of movement and a disorienting musical racket for those who, thanks to drugs, don't even need company. In those days, probably, one of the annoying distractions was to work a little more. Was it really like that? Fenix's grandfather would often say that to heat a room with a stove or feed the fire with logs, you have to warm yourself up several times over: go find it in the forest, gather it, bring it home, chop it, bring it inside, and then, after obtaining the wife's approval, go to the tavern and drink a few glasses of wine from his own batch that he had sold the tavern, and near the gigantic iron stove, in the company of friends, warm up thanks to the wood that others had amused themselves gathering.

Maybe it was different for children. Those of today are born with virtually no need to develop the capacity and the talent of boring themselves. This was not the case with Fenix who, without being able to define what the word "boredom" meant, would only need to stop what he was doing and look up at his surroundings, or go somewhere else to find something of interest.

Once the train left the station, loaded with passengers, including his friend, its loops ended up boring Fenix. Either his mind, or his creativity, had been exhausted. One last turn of the key and the train stopped. He looked at it for a while, sighed, and unconsciously asked himself: "Is that it?"

He looked up and saw the most beautiful picture he'd ever seen, that, like a stamp on his mind, he would never forget. If he didn't know how to appreciate beauty in all its splendour in that moment, the years to come would make him realize it, and in so doing intensify it.

It was Judit, reclined in front of the fire, her elbow on the floor, her cheek in her palm, watching him with her golden eyes that stood out under dark eyelashes, like a cat's; a smile on her lips, which looked as though they were drawn, red, maybe because of the flames dancing around; a tender and concerned smile. Fenix, who had never seen her in this position, stared at her; Judit's free hand played with one of her braids which was already almost undone and her loose hair fell over one of her breasts. She pulled the braids back—her little breast poked out from the neckline of her snow-coloured blouse that was embroidered with a floral pattern. She adjusted it, straightened it, then started undoing the other braid. Every now and then she would stop for a few seconds to detect the first signs of tiredness in Fenix—another yawn, and then a third— so she could bring him to bed without resistance. For Fenix, who didn't understand anything about visual art, it was as though he were in front of a painting whose title could easily have been: *The Birth of a Peasant Venus*, a title that would confirm her slightly bent leg, the hem of her skirt, also embroidered with a circle of flowers, lifted above her knee, both legs with white three-quarter length stockings, without shoes, and her thighs, parted, warm and welcoming. Yes; were it not for her smile that contained a hint of worry, as well as her eyes twinkling in the light of the fire, serious eyes, she would have looked like she was stretched out on the grass in the meadow, on the edge of the forest or on the riverbank. She was only missing a blade of grass or a wildflower in her mouth and the painting would have achieved perfection.

But little Fenix, with the best of intentions, wouldn't have been able to understand the painting's composition, nor when, with the second braid undone, she threw back the second strand and shook her head to fix her thick head of hair; and the peasant Venus's birth was complete.

Although little Fenix wouldn't have understood what the peasant Venus was all about, this didn't stop him feeling his attraction, an attraction that stimulated his creativity. He had seen the ideal tunnel that led to the most beautiful forest in the world and where he most loved to play, and in order to get there, he needed the locomotive. He unhitched it, took it off the tracks to find others that would lead him to the destination he yearned for. On the rug, choo choo, he approached. Surprise and displeasure; as though his locomotive were a vulgar car, the barrier was lowered, the leg that was bent met the other, and, with both thighs glued together, the tunnel disappeared. Fenix looked at her as though she had denied him a piece of his favourite cake. Judit looked back at him. Now her eyes didn't need the flames from the fire: they sparkled on their own and she squinted. Oh, the nature of woman, or of Judit; no wonder there are so many songs about women with brown hair.

As though he were the character from the stories Judit would read him, he pointed with his index fingers and commanded:

"Open, Sesame!"

Nothing happened. He only heard a giggle that he perceived as mocking. The repetition of his command led to the same result. Seemingly faced with something impossible, Fenix waited. Judit sat down.

"Where are you trying to go, little rascal?"

"The tunnel. I want to go into the tunnel."

"Wouldn't it be better if you went into your bed? I can see that you're tired. Come here, in front of the fire. I'm going to put your pyjamas on."

Maybe overloaded with emotions, maybe actually a little tired, or maybe because the command meant moving closer to Judit, Fenix, though grumpy a little about her closing the tunnel, his childhood whim or masculinity, he obeyed like a soldier. Judit crossed her legs so that Fenix could approach her and he, while she took off his shirt and sweater, with his arms up, lowering his head, with his face and nose, took advantage of the opportunity to venture into the valley of the decorated neckline of Judit née Venus's dress, from which emanated odours that stimulated him with new sensations. And in search of others, or in an attempt to delve into these new ones, since she was shaking him a little to remove his clothes, he stuck his head in the silken valley; with his arms raised and somewhat locked, since he couldn't hug Judit, his fighting hands wanted to cling to both her breasts; it was difficult, but Judit, freeing her arms a little, facilitated his task and Fenix's face disappeared into the valley. When he exited from it, pointing toward it, he said:

"Tunnel."

Judit ended up putting his pyjama top on shaking him out of pure pleasure and rubbing him against her. From her laughter came other discoveries, maybe due to pure chance. The neckline wasn't very ample nor were Judit's breasts very big, but with a manoeuvre using both of her hands, she tore the fabric, and both breasts appeared before Fenix's eyes. Without her needing to say a word to him, in his face a mouth, in his mouth a tongue and in his entire body, the ancestral instinct; he knew exactly what to do.

Once more, his attempts at approaching continued to the sound of Judit's panting, which absorbed and exhaled them. She took off his shoes, his pants, and didn't put those of his pyjamas on; it would have been a sin to hide this miracle to which Judit, grateful, gave back all that she had received in her breasts. And at last:

"My little one, my beloved, Sesame is open for you, here is the tunnel for you, come, come find it ..."

Fenix knew nothing of the vocabulary of love. He had never needed it to get to Judit. To his great joy, the tunnel reappeared, her thighs parted, covered by her skirt. He took the locomotive and again, choo choo, and, when he was about to enter, the barrier descended once more. The desire for the initial push was heightened.

Fenix wasn't stupid; in fact, he was smart, although his intelligence wouldn't serve him much purpose in his future life. However, in this case, for the pursuit of his destination, through association, the discovery of one of the variations of the game of hide and seek was useful to him. He put the locomotive aside and, crawling, confronted the tunnel and its barrier.

And this time it wasn't as easy as it was in the meadow or in the kitchen, the resistance was weakening, but slowly, and stronger efforts on his part were required.

"Search, my love, keep looking. It's waiting for you, it's there."

If Fenix was intelligent, when it came to this subject Judit was much more so, maybe even wise. Or maybe it was affection, love, passion for Fenix. She became aware of his tiredness and feared losing him like in a dream. She helped him discover the tunnel and made the clover patch appear, drew Fenix in with a kiss on the mouth and slowly, carefully, she leaned back like the huntress Diana so the arrow wouldn't falter. When she finished lying back, the little miracle promptly lost itself in the silky tuft, as Fenix's head rested between her breasts.

Outside, a world of snow; winter.

Fenix would never remember what had happened exactly. He could speak of a feeling of joy, of a new and different kind of warmth in the moist forest that was intensified by Judit's soft movements and, simultaneously, of a vague sensation, one that was a little frustrating, of having reached the limit, like in a dream, of a hill that he wanted to climb but couldn't. A moist forest that he lost every time he tried to eliminate the frustration he would encounter when he charged with the miracle and which Judit's wisdom put to an end; she delicately wrapped her legs around him and, pressing his head against her naked breasts, with a whisper calmed him: "Fenix, my beloved Fenix, don't move, let me." Judit's movements were almost imperceptible, much more subtle than Fenix's; the first "Ah" came, and the heat around Fenix's miracle intensified.

Outside, winter. No, he would never be able to remember it exactly. It doesn't usually rain in the winter, and it is even less likely to thunder. But thunder shook the window; the glass vibrated. Judit let out an "Ah," maybe not of pleasure, and squeezed Fenix as though she were clinging to him. Her eyes were fixed on the window. She waited as she caressed Fenix's head, which was buried between her breasts. Nothing. She turned her eyes toward Fenix, she raised his head and looked into his eyes. He wanted to draw her in closer so he could kiss her on the mouth, but he could barely brush against her forehead without losing the miracle. Judit loosened a little; softly but skilfully, she helped him navigate toward the door beneath the garden of clovers.

The fire in the fireplace was slowly dying. With Judit's last "Ahhh" he wasn't sure if the trembling was due to his own shudder, to the wonderful pleasure running up his back, to the cold or to the trembling of Judit herself who again had diverted her gaze to watch the window, which now not only vibrated with thunderclaps, but was illuminated by lightning.

Judit lived nearby, and never slept in the palace; she only stayed until Fenix's mother returned. She put one arm around him and stretched out the other, grabbed the coat she would wear to go back to her house and covered little Fenix who was already almost asleep, exhausted from the titanic task that, blessed by the baby Jesus, would be considered his initiation ceremony. And he slept in a winter nest that emanated a heat as pleasant as his feather bed, or even more so. Fenix's warmth also comforted Judit and she tried to sleep. However, the trembling of the glass, her eyes fixed on the window, her fascination with the lightning, impeded her.

The lightning strikes and thunderclaps multiplied. No, he doesn't remember very well. He remembers, yes, that when he woke up, his eyelids heavy, he was already on his feet, staggering a little, his hands on Judit's shoulders as she told him:

"Come now, Fenix, lift your right foot. The right one, I said, right."

She was putting his pyjamas on.

"Now the other."

"I don't want to go to sleep."

"You don't have to go, you're already asleep. Plus, your mother could come back at any moment. If she sees you awake ..."

She fixed the elastic of his pyjamas around him and before lifting him up, she looked at him with her golden eyes, which had now lost their sparkle.

"Fenix, my poor Fenix, what awaits you? What awaits us?"

A kiss on his mouth and he already found himself on Judit's shoulders.

In the bedroom, she put him into the bed. She tucked him in, fixed his hair, kissed him, hugged him.

Fenix: "I don't want you to go."

Judit's eyes sparkled.

"I'm not going. I'll wait until you fall asleep. Or until your mother comes back."

"I don't want ... Oh, I forgot, Judit, I forgot." He sat up in bed. "The train, Judit, the train. I have to put it away."

Tenderly, Judit laid him down again.

"I'll do it for you, don't worry."

"Are you sure? You're not going to forget?"

"No, I swear I won't."

Fenix closed his eyes and opened them again right away. She was still there. The second time he opened them, already almost asleep, Judit was standing at the foot of the bed; a guardian angel. The sounds and voices that were coming from the other part of the house indicated that his mother and grandfather had returned. Now completely asleep, he dreamed of flying angels.

And Judit flew. Not only to put away Fenix's train (his heart pounded with fear), but to correct an oversight. But she was too late. The Mistress had already entered and had discovered the open door of the stove, which she shut with rage. Judit heard the sound of it and once in the living room, disheartened, she also heard what followed it:

"Judit! How can you be so stupid, so careless? Don't you know that with the door of the stove open the heat escapes and more wood is wasted? Look! There's almost nothing left!"

"There's still a lot left. I'll put some more in right now," the grandfather said, from the living room door.

"I didn't ask you for anything. This is an issue and an oversight concerning this house, or rather, Judit. Judit! Tomorrow, come an hour early. The basement needs to be cleaned. Goodnight."

In spite of all of her efforts to remember, now wrapped in her coat and with her boots on, while she made her way from the palace to her house, Judit was certain of having forgotten something, but couldn't remember what.

Before opening the kitchen door, she listened, looked up at the sky, the horizon: neither thunder nor lightning.

It was nothing more than a pause; the front was approaching, little by little, inexorably.

8.

&——**THAT CHRISTMAS NIGHT**, Fenix slept cradled by two warm thighs provided by a beautiful brown-haired golden-eyed girl that not only protected him from the cold that invaded the living room as the fire slowly died, but also from a strange, never before seen winter storm that illuminated the window and made it tremble. It was likely that Judit, upon hearing its sound—the worst way of knowing, knew of its danger and the destruction it could bring, and would still have protected herself, clinging to little Fenix who, although he wasn't yet a grown man, that night had proved that he could one day become one.

In general, although there was no school Fenix needed to attend, but still much for Judit to do, she would usually wake him up early with an initial soft kiss so as not to scare him and whisper his name: "Fenix, Fenix, it's time." Then several kisses on his forehead, nose, sometimes on his mouth, on his neck. "I could eat you up, yes, I could eat you." With tickles all over his body and every once in a while, a nibble. And maybe, without any feelings of guilt, without being consciously aware of it, she would compare Fenix's smell to that of her brothers, or her father, who, in addition to chewing cheap tobacco, would sweat *pálinka* from all his pores.

But the morning after his heroic initiation, Judit did not appear. Fenix, emotionally exhausted, without homework or obligations to ruin his life and disturb his sleep, slept in almost until midday. He jumped out of bed, got dressed in a hurry because of the cold, put his shoes on and, although he knew how to, ran out in search of Judit so she could tie his laces. Anything to be close to her, and, if her blouse was unbuttoned, to see the most beautiful fruits of this earth when she bent over, especially now that his knowledge and playground had expanded since the night before. As he went through the living room door, he remembered the train. Where would Judit have put it? Would she have left the box under the tree? He entered. In the daylight through the window, the Christmas tree remained beautiful, but had lost its magic and enchantment. Fenix looked under the branches, nothing, not even a shadow of the box. Where he thought the tracks would be, they weren't anymore. He looked left and right: nothing. Now he had two reasons to find Judit, his shoes and the train.

With his laces undone, stepping on them, half-tripping, he made his way to the kitchen. Once in front of the door, on the off chance she may be there, he discreetly half-opened it and poked his head in; seeing only his mother with a pot and a ladle next to the table, he began closing it even more discreetly. His mother was a smoker and her sense of smell wasn't as refined as her hearing (she had an excellent ear for music); she heard him, or, simply from the aura of the mysterious waves we emit, she intuited his presence:

"Fenix! Here!"

The powerful, commanding voice, like that of any captain,

stopped the door but didn't cause Fenix to approach; he delivered a smooth: "Yeeeeeessssss?"

"I said come here!"

"I'm looking for Judit. I don't know where the train is and she needs to tie ..."

"Not interested. Tie your shoes and come eat the soup that's been served."

As opposed to in Latin culinary culture, where children hating soup is a classic theme, in Hungarian culture this does not exist. Fenix entered but didn't close the door behind him. On his knees, as he needed to give something in order to obtain something in return, while he tied his shoes, he asked:

"Hmm, what kind of soup?"

"Pea and nokedli."

It was one of the kinds he loved most. For the first time in his life, a struggle took hold in Fenix's heart that until this moment had been unknown to him: between love and food. As it was almost always Judit who served him food, in that ideal combination, he would never ask himself who had cooked it. However, most of the time it was his mother, and Judit was simply an assistant. But Fenix may well not have known that; in his heart, knowing that the soup would take some time to get cold, the desire to see Judit triumphed.

"No! She's cleaning the basement, you'll go after you eat. This afternoon we're moving down there. The bombings might start at any moment."

More due to a lack of vocabulary than a defence of the democratic rights, for which we get worked up in a useless frenzy of words, Fenix, luckily with his shoes now tied, without knowing that it was a dance that existed over in a faraway South American country, began a malambo on the kitchen floor and started crying out. His mother, who had a richer vocabulary but who knew nothing of the sly and subtle modern pedagogical theories, without any fear of failing as a mother, took two steps and grabbed him by the ear. So that his ear didn't get to the chair without him, Fenix followed her. With a push she sat him down at a table that was up against the window and, to calm him like a Christ pinned to the cross, hit him on the head so violently that, like a blessing, reached all the way to his soul.

At this stage in his short life Fenix was already seasoned. He didn't waste time whining or wiping his mucus, but rather, indifferent to his mother's agitation, who was putting things away in a box, drawn by the smell of the steaming soup, since he had already burned himself five or six times, took the ladle and started stirring it and blowing on it. Every little while, as he stirred, he would shoot a glance at the window from which he could see the vegetable garden covered in snow and at the very back, the stable, and Judit's father's adobe house.

Fenix had never had an ear for music, and even less so if one takes into account that at that age he spent his time searching for four-leafed clovers instead of practising scales the way he would with Niki, his first true love as a teenager over in Argentina. However, this does not mean that he didn't have a fine ear for other sounds, especially if they were unusual. How many airplane engines had he heard in his short existence? Not many; they didn't fly over the small city very often. But the whirr that caught his ears' attention, he had no doubt, was that of a plane. Although he would trade all the airplanes in the world for Judit, this didn't stop him from enjoying seeing one. Still stirring the soup (hey, Fenix, careful not to spill it, blows to the head are as infinite as the stars), he was about to ask his mother, who was still just as busy, if he could be excused, when a whistle, soft at first, without a doubt new music that he had never heard before, caught his attention. The whistle increased in volume, the high pitch became painful almost enough to break eardrums but there was no time: the explosion shook the house, and the blast shattered the window into a thousand pieces. In shock, Fenix kept stirring like an automaton the soup full of glass, shards like thin sheets of ice. His mother ran over the pieces that were grinding on the flood; in a frenzy, her eyes searched for shards in her son's: a miracle, she didn't see any. The shards that stay embedded in the soul, just like those of unjust blows to the head, Mother, are invisible.

His mother dragged him toward the basement; this time, he didn't want to lose his arm. He stumbled a few times, but thank God, there were no blows. Rather, his father's ears may have been burning: "For God's sake, when we need him most," "Save his life. Ha. Who would his miserable life matter to? Him, a warrior, don't make me laugh."

In order to access the basement, they had to go out into the open air. They went down the palace's front steps and, under the whirring of the plane engines and more whistling sounds, slipping in the snow, they ran through the back yard. The earth, the basement stairs, shook under the explosions, and, once they were inside, the entire palace threatened to collapse over their heads. As soon as they entered, Fenix, as though he had found his refuge, ran immediately to take shelter in Judit's bosom. She was curled up in a corner; her doe eyes, illuminated by the 40-watt electrical light bulb, sparkled in a manner somewhere between astonishment and terror. How long did the bombing last? Comparing it to eternity wouldn't be an exaggeration. The light bulb went out; Fenix held Judit tighter and she did the same.

The explosions ceased and the whirring engines faded into

the distance. The calm after the storm. They waited in silence for ten or fifteen minutes, during which the silence seemed to amplify. Finally, when cows mooing could be heard, a sign of life, his mother gave the order:

"It's over. Let's go out."

And they went out. Fenix holding Judit's hand. Outside, in the snow, his mother took a few steps back from the palace and inspected it: apart from the broken glass from the kitchen windows, and some of the ones from the veranda, there was no obvious major damage. But what was happening to Judit? Fenix felt her hand crisp around his. He looked up and instead of her, he saw a statue. Her head with open eyes, fixed in one direction: toward her parents' adobe house. Fenix looked that way as well: the house had opened itself into a yawn and, though it was not very clear from this distance, it left its interior exposed like a dollhouse, one that a young girl had made a mess of, not taking care to put things in order.

Although his hand was in Judit's, this time it was Fenix who was holding hers. As they made their way through the snow, the mouth widened and the dolls' outlines were more defined. Her two brothers against the wall, broken, unable to hold themselves up firmly. Her mother on the ground, next to the wood-fired stove; her father, or part of what used to be her father, on the floor between pieces of the table, broken dishes, scattered cutlery, all on a red, dark surface.

Neither Fenix nor Judit had ever taken the foolish and too often hypocritical oath of eternal love. They loved each other, in a strange way; the love of a mother, or a nanny, or a lover, without consciously knowing it: they loved each other. However, at this moment, there was a profound separation: Judit had let go of Fenix's hand and collapsed. Her knees sunk into the snow, in infinite despair; she tried to turn her convulsions, before dying there, into sobs. And Fenix? He was a child, after all. Maybe he didn't even realize that she had let go of his hand and, mesmerized, without knowing exactly what was happening, stared at the dollhouse.

And Fenix's mother? His mother was the first to react. The master's eye the best surveys. She ran into the stable, then ran out looking relieved.

"Luckily the cows and the pig are alright. A divine miracle."

If those words were pronounced by Fenix's mother in that moment or if it is him who is articulating his tongue in an act of vengeance, verbalizing his mother's conduct, he does not know.

The Mistress went to check the henhouse to see if the miracle had taken place there too.

By the time the other neighbours appeared, entering through the gate through which the cows were taken out to pasture, Fenix's mother had already left to run back to the palace. Maybe it was there that the sinister freedom that war provides children with first took root. Fenix, without anyone to take care of him, kept staring. He watched how Judit, after standing up with a howl, stumbled through the ruins, penetrated into that mouth that wasn't called hell although it was, going mad, crying out, "No! No!" running from her brothers to her father then back again, in a circle of madness. Fenix, once his fascination with the scene had passed, vaguely remembers that the desperation in her cries that penetrated his soul contaminated him, and how inside him was building what he now would call anguish; wanting to do the impossible to calm Judit, but he didn't know what to do, except take the shaky hand that his grandfather, who arrived at that very moment, was holding out to him. In the other he held a demijohn of wine.

Two of the neighbours came in and held Judit before, shaking, she sank into insanity. They dragged her outside and Fenix let go of his grandfather's hand: jumping through the ruins, he ran up to her and hugged her at hip-level. Judit, with her eyes full of tears, probably didn't see him, but she ran her trembling hands, red with blood, over his head, down his back, holding him as though he were her lifeline. Fenix, who wasn't even family, was all she had left.

The Mistress, seeing them both dirty with so much blood needlessly spilled, walked away, looking nauseous.

Solidarity, as long as there is war, is limited to the possibility that each of us also feel our problems multiply ... When they saw that Judit, with Fenix leading her by the hand, was headed toward the palace, and the red tracks in the snow that faded as they went along, without having anything to do for the moment, apart from comment on the events, the neighbours went back to their business.

They were probably correct in their conclusions: the plane that dropped the first bomb whose whistle they had heard, without giving the family enough time to find shelter, had fallen on the house, through the thatch roof that seemed intact, had exploded in the middle of the kitchen, more than killing them, shattering them, and the force of the blast had blown the least resistant wall, the one that led to the barn.

That same evening, before they survived another attack, they moved down to the basement. The grandfather had gone into the city with his carriage to stock up on provisions and had waited out the bombing under one of the bridges, clutching a demijohn, deriving strength from his sips. Because of the demands of war—which takes the youngest men, whether married or not, or makes many of them desert, he was practically the only man that was of any use to them. Fenix—still next to

Judit, who moved as though sleepwalking—helped, with the enthusiasm that all change and novelty brings. It was a change, a real adventure that, Fenix would think decades later, today's world thirsts for, turning a trip to the shopping centre and a visit to the Parthenon or the Pyramids into epics. How would he define that distant adventure? At that moment it is impossible for him, but later he could compare it to a gypsy camp or, if not a return to nature, a return to the stone age. In the basement, which was only used as a woodshed or as storage for empty containers that were thrown outside, they went to set up mattresses, blankets, pots and pans, a few pieces of furniture that would end up being useless. From the palace's attic they brought down ham, the *kolbász* that hung from the rafters, the apples that were kept on shelves, a good supply of potatoes of which there were more buried under a layer of hay and of earth covered in snow (a method of preservation now lost and, like the production of sweets, now secret), a bag or two of nuts. His grandfather, with his car, had come back with the same as usual: a few jugs of wine and all the tobacco he would get from the black market.

The power had come back, but only intermittently; for a few hours yes, a few others no. They hadn't brought down the radio, and without the little men, curiously, the darkness seemed to intensify. Luckily, there were candles left. But no one had thought about how, although in the basement they would be protected from the bombs, and although they could effectively keep each other warm like wild animals, it was winter and they had lost that healthy habit of eating raw food, which made their teeth so nice. The grandfather, grumbling, cursing his years, sighing for those during which his sense of smell made him gallop across peaks and valleys in search of a woman, with the help of two neighbours no younger than him, brought over from Judit's a small iron stove and pipes for the smoke, which they took out from one of the basement windows. Its surface would allow them to heat a pot of water, cook a good stew, and incidentally heat their little cave. It was the grandfather who went to get wood and, to bring the water that they had to get from a pump stuck to the demolished house, they took turns.

At the same time as the previous fuss, also loaded with their gear and their provisions (everything up to jars of candy), aunts and cousins arrived. Prepared for the end of the world, there, under the undisputed command of his mother, with his grandfather and Judit, Fenix would live for a year.

According to comments by some who knew, whom his grandfather echoed, the bombing was done by Russian planes, which weren't as effective or precise as the German ones, nor did they have as many bombs as the Americans, whose bombings left no building standing—not to mention humans, who from an efficient perspective had no importance. Not even a rat could survive those so-called carpet bombings; forget rats, they would say, not even a cockroach. The bomb that fell on Judit's parents adobe house, rather than a military objective, although a fatal tragedy, was pure coincidence. Several of the bombs that fell on other houses, in other courtyards and even in the field, didn't explode. This wasn't considered a miracle so much as proof that Russian technology wasn't of the same quality as the Germans'; as a result, there was no doubt that the Germans, thanks to this technology and other miraculous weapons that would appear, would win the war. Very often the expression "It could have been worse" was heard, although it wasn't known what it was referring to.

Before the definitive storm of the front arrived, there were a few days of calm. The living had time to bury their dead. Getting the caskets to bury Judit's family, and others, was a real problem. In Ipolyság, due to the lack of capacity to plan for the future, there wasn't a good stock. For the rare heart attacks, at the back of some carpenter's shop, a spare coffin could always be found, for some client that hadn't yet fulfilled his obligation to pass on to the other side. In general, like local doctors with private practices or those who worked in hospitals, they were missing statistical data and up-to-date information on the subject, and couldn't predict the exact date of death, and the carpenter would make them, made to measure, slowly, following the rhythm of the agony, as much from the cries of pain of the dying person, as the sighs, sadness and delight of the bereaved and the heirs.

There was no shortage of good souls to collaborate in the casket building. Who, in this primitive world where people had to fend for themselves, didn't have a hand-saw, a hammer and some nails, and didn't know how to use them? But, alas, they were missing planks of wood. They remembered Fenix's father's artisanal factory. The front entrance was locked. In a case of force majeure like the war and its dead, and knowing the noble generosity of Fenix's father, it was all perfectly justified to break the lock and take the planks they needed. However, in the presence of the educated and respected Mistress—who, although not the owner of the factory, was at the very least it spiritual co-owner—they requested permission to enter and retrieve a few planks.

There were those who said it was better not to, that it would have been preferable to go inside, take the planks, and case closed. Many other things were said, including comments about Mrs. Jacobowicz's dubious past, since that was the noble last name of Fenix's father's family. Although it was known with one hundred percent certainty that the husband wasn't a "degenerate son of a ...," the wife was subject to all the racist-tinged suspicions that the name carried with it. Upon hearing the request, she screamed to the high heavens, including a threat to go to the authorities, one of whose representatives was in front of her when they asked her permission, and against the advice of her father who was whispering in her ear, the Mistress refused to give up even one plank, let alone several, not even the scraps, because they would be used to feed the palace's fire. Thus, Fenix's mother, through this refusal and future events, not only lost the opportunity to win herself a seat at the right-hand of the Lord, but smeared the family name with a practically indelible stain.

Breaking boxes, with old doors, they managed to build coffins for the dead who were few but, for the small city, far too many. The only funeral home, with a capacity proportional to the frequency of deaths by natural causes, was not enough. Thanks to the help of the volunteer firefighters and their vehicles, various carriages including Fenix's grandfather's (who, with a bottle of wine between his legs, in the front seat brought Judit and Fenix, and in the back, the coffins of Judit's two brothers, since the parents didn't fit in the grandfather's two-wheeled car and were brought instead by a neighbour), the dead arrived at their first destination and found their resting place.

That day, even more than on Sundays or the Day of the Dead, the cemetery was bustling with activity. With Judit holding Fenix's hand, or, given her sadness, he holding hers, they watched and listened to the first sounds of the shovelfuls of earth hitting the coffins of Judit's father, mother, and brothers, which were quieting as the earth piled up and the burial mound was formed, a definitive wall, more solid than one of stone or concrete. The dead, without shadow, without being bothered, could depart in peace and forever travel on the road to infinity as long as they didn't run into the gates of heaven. No one spoke of hell since at this moment it could be found here on Earth. The task of adorning the brand new tombs would be left for later, for better times. A mound of earth and simple wooden cross with an inscription that Fenix would only be able to read later: "Horvath Family." In order not to confuse the dead and to know which belonged to which family, it was the only sign that they left on the graves before leaving the cemetery.

9.

❧——**THERE WERE NO** more bombings, but the front was approaching, and from the basement the sounds of new musical instruments could be heard, some that made the house shake all the way up to the celestial sphere, like Stalin's infamous organ. Also, already known by their sound but never as a tangible, physical reality, the cannon fire, which although they didn't cause as much damage as the bombs, their shells could fall anywhere, like on the mill, when the light went out for good. This new music didn't stop Fenix's mother from worrying about the property. Every second or third day (she was suffering from constipation), she would put on the fur coat, climb the stairs and go into the palace to inspect it. She would look at the furniture, the paintings and the objects of value without finding the answer to the question: where to hide them before the front arrived with the savage Russians? With a finger passed over the surface of a piece of furniture, in a city without vehicles and where the wind only carried pure, white snow, dust of mysterious origin would stick to her and this would irritate her. The house, because of the lack of heating and the kitchen filled with snow entering through the broken window, was frozen. Then she would go into the main bathroom, for her exclusive use. She would never allow her sisters to use it—maybe the one on the veranda if they asked. But in this case, the box attached to the demolished Horvath house would do, and for the children, the entire meadow.

In spite of the cold, she could spend an hour or two in there. Maybe, to comfort herself, she held a genuine clash of the titans. Or maybe not; maybe she lost herself in elaborate fantasies and even, who knows, asked herself how her life ended up the way it did. Did she think of Fenix, of how she treated him? Almost certainly yes, but it was for his own good and it hurt her more than it hurt him. And there was no doubt that she loved him; if not, then why would she give chocolate only to him, as well as the most succulent bits of the casserole. In an hour or two, although fantasies dominated her mind and her reasonings would reduce themselves to mere minutes, she would reach the conclusion that she had the ultimate proof that she was generous: for having welcomed into the palace a father who wasn't one but who ended up better than the real one (well, it depended on how you looked at it; if you were talking about money ...), and in the basement, her sisters or half-sisters. And that is when she found what she was seeking. It didn't take her long to realize that, if she set aside her rage and thought of how good she was, things would be easier for her. And, feeling satisfied, accomplished, she would return to the basement, proud of her benevolence and generosity, feeling and action that she managed to hide effectively enough.

Because she had the most experience, she would send Judit, every day, to feed the cows and milk them, then feed the chickens, geese, and ducks, and collect their milk and eggs, respectively. Whether his mother allowed it or not, and more so if his grandfather went to pet and groom his horse and give a hand with removing the cow manure that was accumulating, Fenix would go along with her. He was the one who would collect the eggs and Judit, without answering a single word, would be reprimanded for the broken ones. The pot on the stove would boil with a chicken or *kólbazs* or a piece of ham, or smoked bacon, potatoes, a bit of salt, and, the same thing that Hitler had provided to each and every German, there would be an egg cooked for each and every one of those who were living in the basement: five cousins, three boys and two girls; two aunts, one widowed and the other with her husband on the front lines or disappeared; his grandfather, Judit, Fenix, and his mother. The owner of the palace and of the basement, a real noblewoman, would manage the food and, like those who think of poor children at Christmas, with eyes moist with pity and compassion, after sighing and uttering: "Lots of people don't even have this to eat" (a very Christian phrase which was echoed by the aunts and that would continue to be repeated until there were only potatoes left) with Solomonic justice, she would give each of them their equal portion. The nuts and apples were for dessert. According to the law stating that charity begins at home, in secret and with the recommendation (probably more of an "order") not to share it, regularly, wrapped in cellophane, Fenix would receive a couple of candies or a bar of chocolate that his mother had hidden since the "Peaceful Days" (which, as the war progressed, would become legend, and no one could remember when they had occurred).

His mother's concern for his physical health, which didn't stop her destroying his soul through his body, without him being conscious of it, produced many conflicts in Fenix's mind; unable to resolve them, he let them sink into the darkness of his subconscious. How they would influence his life in the future, when he would ask himself: "Would it be because my mother …?", he would never really know.

Life in the basement, for the children, wasn't unpleasant. After all, they weren't corrupted by civilization and the cave quickly became their natural habitat. Faced with the permanent external threat, a familial harmony reigned, and there was a marked tolerance toward their mischief. On the rare occasions that things became heated, the undisputed authority of Fenix's mother over her sisters (much more than her father, who, now a grandfather, was cast aside) and their offspring, would quickly put them to rest by shouting a short command. However, the sinister freedom the children had, that had perhaps begun with the first bombing, due to the carelessness of the adults who were busy with other problems or because they considered them old enough to know how to behave, persisted; they would come and go when they pleased and, like Pavlov's dogs with the bells ringing, as soon as they heard the whirring of a plane or the boom of a cannon, they would run to seek shelter. They were even allowed to skate on the lake under the first bridge close to Fenix's palace. Obviously, since the day when they had informed the adults that they had seen a bomb that didn't explode and they were forbidden from touching it, they never told anyone that there had been others and that one of the best forms of entertainment was trying to defuse them and seeing if they could make them explode. They failed every time, and so, either the roar of a plane or of stomachs grumbling (invariably Pavlov) would always send them running back inside right on cue.

Saying that happiness reigned would be an exaggeration; it was nothing more than the children's carelessness, and the adults' worries often cast a shadow over it. What would happen next was a permanent topic of discussion. Moreover, this fear of the future, this constant dread, had produced a weariness that, especially for the aunts, made them go to bed early and silence the military enthusiasm of their children, their pillow fights and the ratata and bang bang of the improvised guns. Fenix's mother and grandfather, the latter of whom smoked his pipe and drank his glasses of wine by the stove over which hung clothes, by the light of a dim candle, kept chatting about who knows what, maybe the good old times or the bad ones. Certainly, those to come.

In order not to fall into total degradation, some rituals were preserved. Putting on pyjamas and nightgowns to sleep, for example. Judit, orphaned, although she was somewhat part of the family, was no more than a luxury slave. In addition to taking care of the farm, she would wash dishes and clean the basement. Exhausted, dead tired, twice as dead because of the emptiness that the loss of her family had caused her, without knowing what her destiny would be (her many tasks gave her time to think of how to free herself from her current one, which could well be definitive), she would finish dinner and excuse herself to go sleep at the back of the basement. As soon as the palace's owner gave the order, "Enough playing. To bed!" Fenix would take the same route as Judit and lie down next to her, on the same mattress and under the same blanket. Once the candle was out, Fenix would search for her to press himself up against her body. Half-asleep or fully asleep, Judit would receive him and put her arms around him and, head against head, a few loving kisses, her only desire was to keep sleeping or to forget her awful life, which was almost the same.

And so, face to face, a gentle push, Fenix's leg would slide between Judit's thighs, protected by her nightgown, his knee would lean against the forest he had so many times adored and they would sleep.

It was pleasant, but with Judit's nightgown and his pyjamas in between them, Fenix wasn't even close to the place he had reached so many times to drink from the fountain of pleasure in the clovers. And even further; as far away as that Christmas night. Whether or not they were lovers was a question of semantics. Fenix had never kissed Judit on the mouth (and why would he?) and she on his not very frequently; the kisses that she had given him on the cheeks, forehead, nose and neck, and those that Fenix had given her on the clover patch, couldn't be considered as authentic kisses of lovers.

Neither Fenix nor Judit had measured the love they felt for one another. But that they adored each other there was no doubt. Fenix, out of fear of blows to the head, pretended to follow his mother's orders to the letter and only gave in to temptation when he was certain that he wouldn't be discovered. Clearly, if the satisfaction and the pleasure promised to be more intense than the pain, nothing would stop him. However, in the case of the chocolate and candies that his mother would give him in secret, as though it were the eleventh commandment, he would follow to the letter. Acting as though nothing was happening, under a blanket, or taking a stroll around the dominion, he would devour them with a certain discomfort. He didn't know what self-esteem was and felt like he was like his mother, or selfish, for not sharing with his cousins.

Who knows why—even he doesn't remember—if it was because of his mother saying "Chocolate gives you energy," seeing Judit so weak, so exhausted, he wanted to give her strength. Or maybe there was some vague dread in little Fenix's soul, maybe the fear of no longer being loved, or that Judit, from thinking of her lost family so much, would soon suffer the same fate as they did. Or, without making too many speculations, simply because he wanted to console her with the fruit forbidden to everyone else, one day gave in to temptation and, like an offering of love, in which everything is permitted, he broke the eleventh commandment.

The discovery of fire and of the wheel remain a mystery. Fenix didn't know a thing about literature about love. He didn't even know how to read and the only stories that he knew were those Judit would read to him, but from them he would never have learned it. It would be another two decades before he got his hands on and understood books such as the *Kama Sutra* or *Ananga Ranga* or *The Thousand and One Nights*. Fenix's discovery was the rediscovery of fire and the wheel.

On that day he ate the candies but kept the chocolate bar. At night, once in bed, Fenix, next to Judit, waited for his mother to put out the candle. Fenix could have taken the chocolate and, as a game or surprise, with his fingers, put it in Judit's mouth, or whispered to her with the voice of lovers, who speak to each other softly, in secret, even in the desert: "Here, this chocolate is for you" so that she could eat it herself. It wasn't forbidden to talk; in fact, after his mother put out the candle, giggles could be heard, voices, grumbles, coughs real or faked, especially among the children. If the sound of cannonballs or other weapons could be heard, they could also resolve their daytime conflicts, but if not, the noise would only last until a "Quiet!" from his mother shut the mouths and all that could be heard were a few whispers until finally only the sounds of breathing or some snoring from the adults remained.

However, to rediscover the fire and the wheel, there are languages that, without pronouncing a single word, not even a moan, are much more effective. The candle out; total silence. Fenix put the bar in his mouth, bit off a piece, twirled it with his tongue, nibbled on it, pushed it against his palate until it softened. He took Judit's head in his hands, directed it in the darkness, and after sticking out his tongue, searched for her mouth. Unaccustomed to this variant, Judit took some time to understand. On the tongue Fenix had stuck out, she perceived the fragrance of the chocolate and as she stuck hers out, with the contact, the taste.

Chocolate, brought from afar, from the ends of the earth, was a luxury item; if not an elixir, at least a delicacy of the gods. But Fenix's mother, to cleanse herself of her sins or to feel good and infinitely generous, every now and then, had given a tiny little piece, some leftover, maybe a little old, to Judit. From a practical point of view, with spiritual consequences, it was somewhat useful to help Judit imagine how beautiful life could be.

Whether it was because chocolate gives energy or not, although she was exhausted, Judit reacted: she gently began licking his tongue; fire had been rediscovered. Fenix's tongue ended up clean; before the delicacy disappeared, he began pulling it in and Judit's followed it to enter his mouth, she explored it, twirling her tongue around several times, signifying the discovery of the garden of delights with her body, the shuddering of which was transmitted to Fenix. The chocolate, the fragrant flowers of the garden, seemed to wither, and, a little disillusioned, she pulled out her tongue without ceasing to press her body against Fenix's; out of gratitude, or love, or both. He bit off another piece, but this one, instead of one or two twirls around his mouth, he put it between his teeth and left a little sticking out from his lips. Only a few movements sufficed so that at a speed just a little slower than lightning, Judit's lips pressed up against his and bit the chocolate. Still with their lips together, Judit felt Fenix push the chocolate, with his teeth partly open, let it pass, made it twirl in her mouth two, three times, and still with lips against lips, passed it to Fenix and he to her and she to ...

And the wheel was rediscovered as well.

How many times it turned that night, doesn't matter.

What matters is that in a faraway country, decades later, some-one who considers himself a common merchant, who counts by hundreds, while (maybe to bring order to the world that he couldn't care less about) he dreams of millions that he claims to despise (or at least those who possess them), his store selling Latin American goods now closed, next to a wood-fired stove upon which he likes to put orange peels to perfume the air, he sips rum in a comfortable armchair, watching the snow fall outside through the window, illuminating the night, he thinks of how if he needed to give a name to the scene of the fire and the wheel, he would call it "The Resurrection of Judit." With the help of the rum, maybe a little bit of hash, he tries to make real what, so many years away, seems to be no more than a dream. Sometimes a sense of pride, a type of aristocratic hon-our inherited from his parents without him realizing it, soothes his sorrows: he never counted the amount of chocolate or candy he had needed (that, moreover, didn't belong to him), for the languor of Judit's body to disappear, to revive this life that, if not beautiful, made the muscles flutter under his skin and pro-duced a warmth that radiated joy. Yes, so that, during the night, there in the basement, thanks to the dessert that pre-ceded sleep, that was real, they found themselves holding each other; he, without his pyjama pants; her, with her nightgown raised. Any closer, more together, or tighter for the caresses, impossible. There was something more, a light breeze, a whis-per of the wind to remember it: Judit's "Ah" that he hears again, but soft, a sigh drowned out by tongues, as though it were pass-ing through his soul. Yes, once more, there in the basement, it was Christmas; but a strange Christmas, certainly. But it was there that for the first time he knew without knowing, rocked by Judit's gentle movements and her final clasp, what it is to be one with the universe.

How many times these nights repeated themselves, doesn't matter either. All things come to an end. What mattered was that Judit would start humming when she would go milk the cows, feed them, and collect the eggs with Fenix. His mother's reproaches about them taking too long, didn't matter to either of them. The excuse that the hay was further and further at the back of the stable, far from the trough, was a sufficient reason to justify the tardiness, and if they rolled in the hay, a variant of love or a simple game provoked by the happiness that arose out of who knows where, they didn't need to explain.

And slowly, as the days became longer, the thaw began, as did what they had been waiting for to signal the end of this story so they could return to normal life, but, with the best of intentions, Fenix would never know what it was: the front had arrived.

—✤ 10.

✤—**THE CANNON FIRE** ceased and other new music appeared: the rattling of machine guns, gunshots, screams and howls in the street. The Germans had already emptied his father's artisanal factory of all things iron and were stealing more iron from all around, including, a sacrilege, several of the crosses from the cemetery. The only task they had left was to escape. Sometimes, Fenix's grandfather, carefully half-opening the front gate of the courtyard, would venture out. He would return running, frantic, either from the effort or the urgent need to report back. Outside, the Apocalypse: vehicles full of human remains, bleeding men, with reddened bandages, mutilated, half-blind, amputated, with their heads caved in, running through the streets searching for their graves. Many of them fell just about anywhere, without having settled on a location for their eternal slumber. The Russians were ruthless; their cleansing operation's motto was "Never forgive, never forget." The discipline and lively singing that the Germans had arrived with before heading off to the front turned into screams; a panicked and hopeless rout.

Silence; once more, silence. He who recalls history remembers no silences more sinister than those of war. It isn't the silence, those few seconds or that minute, of the morning before sunrise, or before sunset, before the birds and other critters of the night begin the activity for which they were created; the mosquito's buzz, the cricket's chirp. Nor that of the desert, where there seems to be no sign of life; only the howling wind. The silence of two o'clock in the afternoon in torrid countries or of two o'clock in the morning, when the entire universe seems asleep and the meteorites that enter into the atmosphere make no sound. Nothing to do with the silence imposed by his mother, on him and the others in the basement. Not even the infamous and often studied silence of the poet behind words, that no one understands but about which anyone can give themselves the luxury of thinking and rambling on about at their leisure. And even less so the definitive peaceful silence of cemeteries. No, the silence of war is charged with threats, like the second before the triggers are squeezed on the guns of the firing squad; or it can be even stranger (Fenix will never forget it): in the total, almost absolute silence, the dragging of the feet of those they would bring to the station, his friend among them. The cry that would have broken that silence with his name was held back by Judit.

Yes, a strange, different kind of silence. One night, this night, the command: "Silence!" didn't come out of his mother's mouth. Just when she was about to speak it, upon noticing the other silence, she contained herself; it seemed as though she breathed in so as not to let out even a letter while, slowly, they all realized and that the silence they were hearing was growing until an explosion more violent than any bomb shook the earth, making the palace's foundations tremble.

And once more silence; everyone knew what would happen next and waited. They waited ten, fifteen minutes, but the second explosion, closer to the city, arrived like an echo in the distance. However, since the bridge was bigger, and required the most potent of the invention of he who bequeathed to humanity the Nobel Prize, not only would the Virgin in the square have trembled, but it would even have reached Jesus on the cross of the Calvary. From there, maybe, the echo.

The Germans, to slow the Russians' advance, blew up the bridges over the lake and river. And they did something more: they cut the path for Fenix's grandfather's wine and tobacco supply; anyway, it had been some time since anyone could find the latter anywhere and, when the stock had been exhausted, he would resign himself to smoking dried corn silk.

That night, once the cleansing operation on that side of the river was complete, the silence that followed would not produce any danger or surprise. The thaw had already made the river overflow and with the bridges demolished, the triumphant march of the Russians was stopped. It would seem that before the final onslaught to take the city, the Russians decided to rest, as well as the inhabitants of the basement—without needing the mother's order—along with all the basement dwellers of the surrounding area.

Pondered during nightly insomniac worrying sessions, dreamed in nightmares, or, upon waking, shared aloud, the inevitable question, every morning: what would happen next? That morning, as though there were some imperative necessity, as though they did so every day, or as though it were Sunday and they needed to go to church, there was another question: now, without the bridges, how would they get to the city? A strange new feeling: the city was there but unattainable; from the veranda one could see it over the brick wall that protected the palace from only God knows what, since not even a tower was left standing from the edge of the plot where the Horvath family house stood with its yawn, as well as the stable where, at this moment, Judit was arriving with a bucket and Fenix with a basket. Before entering, hand in hand, they looked toward the city. Yes, it was there: like in a fairy tale, reflected on the surface, it seemed to be floating adrift in the flooded river. In the field, the water encroached on the palace's grounds. While they watched, the grandfather joined them, as he had just finished his task of shovelling manure. The three of them stared; the grandfather with some sniff-sniffing sounds that caught their attention. Judit and Fenix looked at him; seeing the tears in his eyes, Fenix let go of Judit's hand and held his grandfather's.

"What's wrong, Grandpa? Why are you sad?"

His grandfather's voice sounded broken:

"Never ... it will never ... be the same. Those bridges ... they ... were 300 years old. It was like ... like they were ... my ancestors that ..."

He dried his tears with the sleeve of his jacket, turned, let go of Fenix's hand and went into the stable.

Around noon, as the pot boiled on the stove, violent pounds could be heard on the front gate. Silence. Again the pounding which now, multiplying, resounded like a drum circle. The Mistress yelled: "They're going to knock it down! Let's go!" Doubts, worries, fears, hesitations, shouting outside. All together, with the grandfather leading them, left the basement, wondering what else, what else, until, when they reached the gate, some of the boards of which had begun to loosen under the force of the blows with the rifles. "They're going to break it down! Do something, for the love of God!"

Along with the pounding, with laughter and cries of encouragement in a language with a familiar accent, the gate received the pounding, which made the planks of wood split and crack. In turn, the grandfather, after approaching, taking hold of the bar, and catching his breath, delivered a few "Stop! Stop!" cries in Slovak, cries that he needed to repeat until he heard the pounding start to quiet.

And he lifted the bar.

As soon as they half-opened one of the doors of the gate, the barrels of two or three machine guns appeared along with several other guns. Slowly, the door kept opening; more machine guns, more guns, and with the door completely open, behind the guns appeared the front made flesh: bearded, gaunt, dirty soldiers, with their uniforms—if that is what they once were—torn to shreds, blood on their faces, a bandaged eye, heads wrapped in bloody dressings, legs fastened to splints, arms in slings. A large group of men who, upon seeing who appeared behind the open gate, lowered their guns against their chests, and silence, as they contemplated without any of the soldiers or anyone from the house making a single move. It was as though they were all searching for the answers to questions that weren't formulated, those of the house: What were they doing here? What did they want? What could they give to this horde that seemed to have come from another world?

The horseshoes resonated on the pavement. Four or five of them appeared on horseback, and stopped behind the line of soldiers. "Cossacks!" the grandfather exclaimed. The riders, well dressed and clean, clean-shaven, with ironed uniforms, fur hats, sabres hanging from their belts and machine gun cylinders over their shoulders, as though a movie were being filmed and they were the stars, with fierce looks on their faces, bucking a little until one of them called out and the line of soldiers was split into two to let them pass (those of the house understood the call and automatically followed the soldiers' movement), and they passed through them as well.

When the Cossacks—because they were—reached halfway across the courtyard, not only had the bucking of the horses stopped, but they were also gripping their machine guns. Two of them disappeared behind the courtyard of the palace; one, like in a circus performance or a movie shoot, made his horse climb the front steps of the palace; another, of only seventeen or eighteen years of age ("A child," someone said), pointing them with the barrel of his machine gun, still with a fierce look on his face, frowning, examined the group one by one and stopped at Judit, whom he looked up and down as if she were hiding a ton of grenades. Fenix felt Judit tremble, in fear, or maybe pleasure for having caught the eye of a young man—a Cossack on horseback, no less—whom she would also have liked to climb up and ride with, so gallant, a handsome lad of her age, more or less. This he remembers today, of course; in that moment, although the feeling of jealousy had already awakened in him and he knew it well, he thought it was nothing more than fear. And before the Cossack followed an order that thundered in the air, he learned what a wink was—part of universal sign language—when the Cossack shot one Judit's way and she, blushing, put her head down. If the pinch that Fenix felt was of jealousy mixed with confused rage, the little Cossack would need to meet his punishment that, truth be told, although in this moment she brought him joy, his memory brings him no pleasure at all. On the contrary.

He stops at the words "movie shoot." And there is some truth to that; he remembers and relives that era like a daydream very similar to those that movies often produce. So much so that sometimes he wonders if it even happened. Well, he would like to believe it. And others, as though they had multiplied, or accumulated over the years that had passed, the totality of the memory weighs so heavily on him that he can barely get out of bed— though maybe he doesn't want to, because he considers it useless.

More shouting, more commands. Two Cossacks dismounted, followed by four or five soldiers, then climbed the stairs and entered the palace, blowing off the lock with a machine gun blast. The Mistress cried out, but no one heard her. The other door of the gate didn't suffer a better fate; it would have sufficed to lift the bar that held it onto the ground and it would have opened as though it were oiled. But no, this isn't how men do things: ten or fifteen jumped up against the door of the gate and *crack*, it opened so spontaneously that two or three of them rolled onto the floor. A nudge from Fenix's mother made him hold in his laughter. In the end, one of the Cossacks, with his sabre tapping against the side of the horse, left in a rush and they, still in the courtyard, having forgotten the pot that they had left boiling over the fire, watched with astonishment as ten or fifteen minutes after the disappearance of the Cossack, trucks and vans arrived, from which emerged an almost endless line of stretchers of wounded, of soldiers with crutches, who were entering the palace and behind them, closing ranks, doctors, nurses wearing white coats and carrying metallic boxes full of instruments. Within an hour, the palace, to the Mistress's horror, had been converted into, if not a hospital, then some kind of recovery sanatorium. And thus, with a permanent guard armed with a machine gun next to the wide-open gate, with vehicles that sometimes entered and others that were parked in the street, they brought more wounded and sick.

But for this to have been possible, since several patients were arriving every day, as big as the palace was, they had to make room for them. Fenix and his cousins were always loitering in the courtyard and as they watched the wounded enter, those who left through the gate never to return seemed to be in better health than when they had entered. How could they tell? Without knowing if they were the same ones, they had no other marker than the cleanest dressings that they came out with or instead of walking with two crutches, with just one, or none, or they were barely limping. He remembers the first day when everyone had already gone to eat and they pulled out a soldier with his uniform and boots on. They lay him on some gasoline tanks stuck to the walls and there they left him with his eyes open, looking up at the blue of the sky that seemed to have gotten in his eyes. Fascinated, Fenix stood there studying him, asking himself impossible questions. He remembers that he would leave and come back several times to see if he was still there, including one time when, pulling her by the hand, he brought Judit with him to show her the soldier with open eyes and who, like an obsession or terrorized fixation, with his eyes fixed, he continued to stare at the sky. Pointing him out, he asked her various questions:

"Why is he there? What is he doing? What is he looking at?"

He felt a squeeze of his hand but didn't hear an answer. Giving her a tug on the arm, he delivered a pressing:

"And?" and he looked at her.

He regretted it immediately. Her lower lip was between her teeth and from her eyes fell two tears that rolled over her cheeks. She dropped her lip and answered him:

"He's sleeping."

And he:

"Sleeping? With his eyes open? Come on, don't lie to me, how can you sleep with your eyes open?"

In his life he had never seen a smile so bitter; and if he had seen it, he wouldn't have noted it as such nor would he have understood nor would it have reached his soul (or it may have only reached it just now):

"Fenix, my little Fenix, when you sleep forever, it doesn't matter if your eyes or closed or not."

The bitterness had disappeared from her smile when she told him:

"Let's go eat, Fenix. The soup must be hot again but the potatoes are mashed."

It wasn't the first dead person little Fenix had seen in his life, far from it; apart from Judit's parents and brothers in the first bombing, he had seen others, killed by cannon or shell fire. However, this was the first that stayed etched (or maybe it would be better to say sown) into his soul and that, later on, would bear too many bitter fruits; on that day he learned that there are many ways to drink the infinite or travel to no avail in search of its limits.

He left with Judit to go eat. As soon as he received the chocolate (there were no candies left, but the chocolate was enough for him), he put it in his pocket and ran to go see the soldier. He was still there, but seemed more rigid to him, harder, as though, despite being dead, his life and maybe his soul were abandoning him and, rather than flying, they had evaporated up to the blue sky beyond which could be found the beginning of the path with no end. Maybe this was what gave him the impression that his eyes were more opaque.

The soldier stayed in the same place all night. The next morning, when Fenix arrived at his side, he didn't see boots. Someone, another soldier, or one of the neighbours who had now started wandering around the area, must have needed them more.

Around noon, four soldiers arrived with two shovels. They put the dead man on a stretcher, passed in front of the stable, the yawning house, and brought him to the back of the yard, a few metres from the waters of the rising river. And watching that burial from afar—he would always remember it as *that burial*, during which they covered the dead man's eyes with eyelids made of earth, he would have thought that it was the burial of an unknown soldier, the only real one of flesh and blood that would dissolve in the ground without anyone bringing him a flower; they didn't even mark his resting place with a cross. Yes, *that* burial and not another, like the famous one in France and other cities, so useful for beautiful ceremonies of washed consciousness, for a distant war, for adultery, for the sale of weapons: a public confessional.

The little city that, liberated by the Hungarians, had recovered its former name from the Peaceful Days, Ipolyság, with the arrival of the Russians, although they hadn't yet taken the main part, took back its old Czechoslovak name of Šahy. But Ipolyság or Šahy, although not the Indies that Columbus discovered with a handful of galley slaves, was re-conquered; if not by galley slaves, then by prisoners liberated from jails, a group of criminals, thieves and, who knows, maybe murderers. How people knew this, no one is certain, but it is possible that from that knowledge emerged the legends of lootings and rapes— even an eighty-year-old woman, raped by fifteen soldiers, one after the other, and if there were only fifteen of them it was because at that number the poor old woman passed away and became the unknown rape victim, feminist heroine and martyr, although the act was never proven. However, there were indeed violent acts, and Fenix himself would drink from this bitter cup.

While the Russians prepared for the invasion and total conquest of Ipolyság (now once again known as Šahy)—not at all an easy task due to the rising river and the absence of the bridges), with the sanatorium operating over their heads—the family carried on living in the basement.

Everyone had to admit it: it was lucky that the palace had transformed into a hospital or sanatorium and not into a pigsty where soldiers lived huddled together like cockroaches. The doctors, in addition to being professionals, were learned men, or seemed like it. But Fenix's mother wasn't reassured. Not only did she feel rage and fury upon seeing her dominion invaded by rude and disrespectful strangers who forbade her from using the bathroom when she needed to (she needed only think of her squatting position in the Horvath family outhouse to turn red in the face), but, furthermore, from what she had heard about the troops, without it occurring to her that the doctors may be different (if they were actually doctors and not butchers like the rest, according to her), she was concerned for the fate of her paintings, china, rugs, crystals and who knows what other knick-knacks, as a stoic philosopher would say, like her clothing, except the otter skin coat that she had hidden in the basement and in which, wrapped in her dignity, gathering courage, she climbed her palace stairs to find out what in God's name was happening in there, behind the broken windows covered with the first piece of rubbish they could find, and what was left of her treasures and riches.

Fenix's mother, of Hungarian lineage, the only member of her family with a bachelor's degree, had a respectable knowledge of German, but, since she considered Slavs to be inferior beings, apart from "Da" or "Niet" in Russian, she didn't speak a word of any Slavic language. Her father, Fenix's grandfather, did not hold these prejudices; furthermore, as a merchant carried by the sails of trade, or drawn by some subtle and adhesive perfume of the distant sirens, he needed to know at least some basic Slovak in order to undertake commercial or amorous negotiations. However, to Fenix's mother, the grandfather, with his lambskin coat, white whiskers stained with nicotine—same as his teeth, of which he was missing a few—didn't seem to her to be the right person to represent, even as a mere interpreter, the stock she believed she belonged to thanks to her marriage or (she was a woman, after all) just because. Convinced that the Russian doctors, although they were doctors, didn't speak Hungarian or German (language of the enemy) she resorted to little Fenix, who had picked up Slovak without even realizing it, from playing in the street, and who she had seen speaking fluently with some soldier or Cossack who was wandering around the courtyard. Dressed in her fur coat and pulling Fenix—with his face washed, his hair combed, wearing a white shirt and just a thin jacket, shivering from the cold— along by the hand, she climbed the stairs to her dominion with controlled fury, but not so controlled that Fenix didn't risk losing his footing and falling down if his mother hadn't yanked on his arm.

The Mistress was what one would call well put together. Not only sophisticated, but also tall and elegant. And so, after knocking on the door of her own palace, with the lock still broken, the doctor (or rather nurse, it seemed, from his air and the red band around his arm) who opened the door to them, perhaps propelled by his own necessity, or by the association with a woman so proud, wearing a fur coat in a war so bloody and miserable, with the world's oldest profession at the service of some officer, gave a conceited and complicit smile, a smile that he wiped from his face the moment he noticed Fenix, a child, an almost sacred object for Russians. Fenix understood the greeting and the words that followed.

"What did he say?" Fenix's mother asked him.

"He said 'Hello' and asked what we want."

Fenix translated. The other one asked on whose behalf. The owner of the palace. One moment, please. They closed the door. The time·they needed to wait (ten minutes?) seemed to the Mistress to be an eternity and a humiliation of her nobility.

There is no doubt that in war, or in *this* war, not everyone went hungry. The doctor who opened the door wasn't fat, but neither his body nor his face (with his nose a little red) manifested the hollow, sunken features typical of malnutrition. He was a head shorter than the Mistress. With little possibility of error, it could be guessed that the doctor had taken time because he was changing his smock, since the soft reddish colour of the bloodstains were barely noticeable on the one he was wearing; or, he was eating, after a few preliminary shots of vodka, which was highly likely since as soon as he opened his mouth, the Mistress (undoubtedly a visceral reaction that she couldn't help) scrunched up her nose and threw her head back. Thank God, the doctor didn't seem to notice; he had bowed and with a ceremonious greeting, accompanied by a gesture with both arms, invited her in.

Fenix's mother entered the palace with the dignity of a queen before an intruder; her chin up, so much so that the upper half of her eyes needed to be completely white for her to see where she was stepping. In the entrance hall, Fenix saved her from tripping on the cot of a soldier with a bandaged head. Whether because of the smell of formaldehyde, of alcohol, or of vodka (the preferred Russian remedy for all ills), in order not to trip or step into a puddle of blood, his mother soon abandoned her queen-like posture to walk carefully but with a nauseated look on her face that she couldn't hide. The doctor, repeating every so often the word *kultura*, which didn't require translation, followed her and tried to direct her although the Mistress, in a half-sleepwalking state, as though she were walking through hell, paid him no mind. Once in the living room with the stove and the piano, the Mistress kept pacing between the furniture, the sofas, the armchairs covered in sheets to protect them but which, with all the wounded soldiers, some of whom were bleeding like Christs, would be difficult to save from being stained with the vital fluid. In addition to the armchairs and sofas, there was no shortage of beds in multiple bedrooms; they had to circulate in the makeshift aisles between the large number of cots. Fenix does not know if it was because of the stains that could be seen on the floor or if it was in order not to brush against the edges of the cots that his mother, with both hands, raised her coat as though she were walking through a muddy area full of branches with bloody rags hanging from them. But the last straw was when they got to the master bedroom; aside from the cots, the marriage bed was full of piled up wounded, including, as their skirts and naked legs revealed, women soldiers. Whether his mother's shriek was due to her horror at the sight of her bed soiled with blood and the dirt from their boots, or if it was because of her moral indignation at the promiscuity of mixing women with men, was unclear. It could easily have been both. Only decades later, when Fenix would learn the full meaning of the word *hypocrisy*, remembering this shriek, would he understand what it really meant.

For the moment, the open eyes of the wounded who were already awake, and of those who were awakened by her shriek, fixed their eyes on his mother who, as though the beams of their stares had materialized and she had been hit by them, staggered. The doctor, probably already sick of repeating the word *kultura* without her paying attention to him, without ceasing to repeat it, took the Mistress by the hand and one step to the right, another forward, another to the left, he directed her to the bathroom attached to the master bedroom, the one she was prohibited from using for her meditative retreat.

The bathroom as such had almost disappeared. However, what it was hiding and what his mother saw there served as a rain of solace over her spirit, body, and soul. The deep sigh of relief that she emitted proved it. Perhaps, worried about the puddles of blood she was stepping in, when she had entered, she didn't even notice the missing rugs and even less the walls without a single painting hung on them. The word *kultura* rung out once more and Fenix was able to translate a few fragments of his rambling: that they were well-educated people, who knew how to care for objects of value, that they appreciated the art and this was why they had taken down the paintings and stored them into the bathroom. And as he spoke, he lifted the sheet that was covering the paintings. Lined up against the wall, the columns, and in a basket on the toilet, as though they had been guillotined, the heads of Liszt, Petofi, Goethe, and others. He showed her the Persian rugs rolled up and covered in sheets. He uncovered the sink in which he had put porcelain and crystal miniatures, then covered it again quickly since many of them were broken. The same manoeuvre with the bidet. In another basket, under the sink, flatware and silverware. But that was all the doctor needed to do. Fenix translated the question:

"Madam, is everything in order?"

"Da!" the Mistress answered, with the enthusiasm of someone speaking their native tongue.

Toward the exit, guided by the doctor, they crossed the living room. The Mistress, who wouldn't settle for little, was undoubtedly satisfied with the safe-keeping of her most prized objects— if not all of them, at least the majority. And that satisfaction made her forget that she had a skirt and a fur coat to protect. Letting them fall, she crossed the room and her eagle eyes, from up above, shot looks right and left, over the cots, inspecting the walls, the stove, and— when her gaze landed on the piano, she gave an astonished, "Oh!" and stopped short, went pale, extended her arm and with her index finger trembling with indignation, pointed to a hammer and sickle that had been beautifully engraved into the black lacquer of the piano and underneath, some incomprehensible writing. The doctor, who had gotten ahead of them, retraced his steps. He observed attentively the direction of the finger and shook his head as though surprised by the Mistress's lack of *kultura*. He approached the piano, leaned over a little, and one by one pointed and spelled out the Cyrillic characters underneath the hammer and sickle. He then stood upright and pronounced the full sentence, which Fenix, now familiar with the phrase, having heard it several times each day from the soldiers and Cossacks, translated it thus:

"Long live Comrade Stalin."

The word that the Mistress pronounced was incomprehensible; to contain it, she had to bite down with rage. She didn't need the doctor to show her out, she knew her way around her property; Fenix needed to run to catch up to her and go down the stairs behind her.

And life carried on. It's true that many wouldn't call it a life, and even less so in the basement, but what is certain is that for Fenix and for Judit, nightfall, when his mother blew out the candle, meant it was time to interweave and bury themselves in the most delicious nest that could be found on this earth. The chocolate had run out but they had already forgotten about its existence. There are better, more sublime flavours. Most of these episodes began with the mutual intertwining; sometimes they slept that way. Other times, after the mutual exploration, while squeezing each other tight enough for their souls to unite, they would move on to other games: either Judit could search with her fingers to provoke the miracle and afterward draw Fenix between her thighs to offer him the warmth of the clover patch under the sun, or Fenix would lead the search for the four-leafed clover, the way he had done in the kitchen, or in the grass of the meadow, or in the shade of the trees of the forest.

It was likely that, for Fenix, who quickly adapted to his new circumstances and grew in harmony with the miracle, his living situation—with his taste for adventure, in a primitive cave, while outside wandered dinosaurs—was the ideal, was absolute perfection, and there was no reason why it shouldn't be eternal. For some time now, without asking for more explanations that Judit wouldn't give him, he had adapted to those four or five days during which Judit would forbid his excursions into her territory, and instead, would dedicate herself to Fenix's, to his great delight. That variation gave way to the first steps toward a reign in which he would be served regularly like a king, but its glory would never be matched, nor would it extend to a larger territory, except in illusions or fantasies.

And they carried on living, largely on potatoes. It would never be known exactly how, but the event occurred: although the Mistress, in the first bombing that killed Judit's family, considering it a blessing from God, was happy that the cows were spared, the Jacobowicz farm remained deserted. Perhaps, at night, it was the good neighbours that they greeted with a smile during the day, or prowlers who had come from other parts in search of treasure, in a marvellous world in which an egg can be turned into a gold coin. Maybe not; maybe it was nothing more than the necessity of supplying the hospital and in so doing feed some hungry soldiers. Fenix and Judit saw how, after killing it with a decisive blow, three or four Cossacks butchered one of the cows with slashes of their swords, and several soldiers carried its parts toward the palace. Perhaps because it resembled Rocinante too much, only the grandfather's horse was left. However, the hunger reached the point where, to save him, the grandfather slept in the stable at night.

As much as Fenix's mother rationed the food, without the farm's provisions, the ham, the *kolbász* and all the protein very soon disappeared. Once an adult, Fenix would tell a friend that his psychological issues weren't only due to the fact that he was born, according to his mother, with a flattened skull, but rather that he spent a year eating potatoes that were dug up at night. And since in those days science hadn't yet discovered the fabulous vitamin complex that this tuber contained, and that it is actually recommended to eat them with the peel, just as he had eaten them, without knowing it, he probably believed he had eaten potatoes with no vitamins, an easy justification for his future foolishness.

There was a surprise, not so much in Fenix's exterior life as in his interior one, interior that he only knew a little, unconsciously, through the infinite happiness and security that Judit offered him, through the fear and hatred of his mother, through his empathy with the sadness and pain for the death of Judit's brothers and family, through the loss of his friend, through the joy of riding in his grandfather's car, through the pleasure of playing in the street with his other friends, and, without counting the toys per se, like the train that he remembers every once in a while and that no one knows about, that was more or less it, and this was not insignificant: it was his entire life, which would soon be completed, or expanded, with some torturous conflicts.

The divisions that arrived in the little city were not exactly the best of the best of the Soviet troops. The Cossacks were a strange, mounted squad, separate from the army, always in movement, coming and going on mysterious missions. The words *Cossack* and *horse* were almost interchangeable. Fenix always saw them, up there, and, sometimes, without them dismounting, in spite of the bucking of their horses, he would manage to engage in a brief dialogue with one who, grabbing him by the hands, would lift him onto his horse, adjust him on the saddle and, while gripping the mane, Fenix would go for a ride with him. Once the ride was over, he would take him down and the bucking would resume. If Judit came to get him, for example, the bucking would noticeably increase, the rider would smooth his moustache, and, as though pride or fear didn't fit inside of him, with two kicks of his spurs into the horse's stomach, he would disappear on a highly important mission.

Cossacks could never be seen on guard duty anywhere. Those who stood guard at the hospital's front door weren't exactly diplomats. Generally, they were Krygyzes, who didn't always walk with a firm step, and, according to Fenix's grandfather, at night, they often needed the support of the rifle or, if they had machine guns, the doorpost of the gate.

And one night, one of them, abandoning his post, went down to the basement. The only people still awake were Fenix's mother and grandfather, who were chatting; the latter was about to retire to the stable to watch over his horse. Both of them went silent when the Kyrgyz appeared at the foot of the stairs. That he was drunk, they had no doubt. It was well known that Russian soldiers drank more than they ate. Whether or not the Mistress, thinking that he was hungry, made a mistake in offering him a cold potato, will never be known. The Kyrgyz may have taken it as an offering of love and, called by another kind of hunger, pushed her, making her fall to the floor. The grandfather wanted to intervene; his bones creaked when he felt him drive the butt of the machine gun into his chest. It was an absolutely convincing argument: it winded him, folding him in two. With the grandfather eliminated, Fenix's mother, paralyzed, mesmerized by the situation, watched as the Kyrgyz undid his pants, lowered them, and without forgetting the instruction never to abandon his weapon, with the machine gun still hanging from his shoulder, he pounced on her.

He didn't get very far. With a desperate howl that still resounds in his ears today, Fenix jumped out of bed and charged at the assailant, kicked him, hit him, as he screamed and screamed. It was not only a legend that Russians adore children; it was a reality Fenix had proven several times. But it appears that Kyrgyz wasn't aware of this adoration. He warded him off with a push but Fenix, innocent and reckless, resumed his attack. The Kyrgyz decided to stand up, grab Fenix and toss him to the back of the basement. Fenix rolled over the mattresses between his cousins and aunts. Dizzy, now with tears in his eyes, he tried again and charged once more.

Chance occurrences, in war, are infinite; maybe just as much as, if not more than, in the life that we still call *normal*, but the results and consequences tend to be different. No one, neither Fenix nor any of the people in the basement, saw the officer standing halfway down the stairs with his pistol drawn. He shouted once and the Kyrgyz stopped and froze. The officer finished his descent and, still pointing his gun, approached him. He took his machine gun from him, and, given the action that followed, he seemed to have given the order of pulling his pants back up. The officer hung the machine gun from his shoulder and approached Fenix's mother; he helped her to her feet. In the language that she didn't understand, he calmed her, consoled her, and from what Fenix could understand, and probably the grandfather too (although neither of the two said nor translated a word), he asked her if she wished for the rapist to be punished. It was likely that the officer attributed the Mistress's blushing to her modesty as a fragile woman, rather than to her embarrassment for not having understood even a single word of what the officer was saying to her, or to something that had unsettled her deep down to her obscure core. And so, now recovered a little, perhaps wanting to conceal her ignorance and make a good impression, she delivered two enthusiastic *da, da*. The officer bowed, clicked the heels of his boots together and left with a "Goodnight" in Russian.

Shoving him with the pistol in the back of his neck, he brought the Kyrgyz with him. With the door of the basement closed, the sound of feet dragging could be heard, slowly quieting; then, silence, a silence that intensified like before a fatal leap in the circus— a silence that was pierced by the discharge of a machine gun.

It was unclear whether the shot was a summary judgment from Fenix's mother's *da, da*. Since Fenix wasn't nor would ever be sure of whether the oblique eyes which, the following day, around back, near the water that was encroaching onto the terrain, looking up at the sky, waiting to be covered in dirt, belonged to the same Kyrgyz.

His mother never thanked her son with an embrace, a caress, or even a simple "Thank you." She only mumbled a few incomprehensible words at him. Given the state her son was in, only decades later would he would grasp their meaning and weight.

It was Judit who, that night, embraced Fenix's trembling

body with more affection than ever before. The feeling of adoration for his mother, which arose in him for a few minutes as he
tried to save her, was completely unknown to Fenix, who, on the
surface of his consciousness, only felt rage and, every so often, a
wave of hatred. The adoration would bury itself again, the rage
would be reinforced and the waves of hatred would come back
more frequently with feelings unknown even to this day: the
guilt for hating her, and the guilt for being unable to adore her.

Decades would pass and a moment would arrive when, once
what his mother had mumbled to him had become clear, the
guilt for having hated her would be revived. It was at the end of
a goodbye, maybe a final goodbye. His mother put a plastic
tube in his hands, the kind that hold university diplomas, and
told him: "Do you remember that time you tried to save me
from being raped by the Kyrgyz, and I promised you that one
day I would make it up to you? Well, in this tube you have a
hundred Mexican gold coins. It's for my grandchildren but, if
you find yourself in a predicament, you can use them." Fenix
took the tube: its shape and weight reminded him of the shells
they used to play with in the field.

Yes, the guilt for having hated her would be revived, but not
the guilt for having been incapable of loving her. The struggle to
stop gravity from swallowing the tube, carrying his soul with it,
must not have let him. Or perhaps it was worse: the shame of
having accepted it. And worse yet, not having the courage to give
it back. Could it be true that he really was like his father, as his
mother never tired of repeating to him? Maybe she had told
him too many times. Hopefully, it was nothing more than that.

Spring had fully arrived. The thaw had ended and, like every
year, the water from the river flooded the terrain at the edge of

the property and almost reached all the way to the stable. We always speak of the rebirth of nature; this time, this Spring, one could speak of the rebirth of the war, an advancement of the front; brief, but a rebirth all the same.

Life is strange, including war, with the way its episodes are discussed as though it were a football game, or a horse race. And since they were no longer in the Middle Ages, no one spoke of the art of war, and no one compared it to a game of chess. It was discussed, yes, because the Russians didn't take advantage of the winter, when the river was frozen and they could have skated over it. They acted as though they had more than enough people to make their attack in the spring, and in the middle of the day, so that the twenty or thirty Germans strategically located with cannons and heavy machine guns could defend the city as comfortably as they would a medieval fortress. There was no shortage of comments asserting that the delay was most likely due to the fact that the Russians didn't have skates. On the infamous military intelligence, producer of absurd tactics. The order to invade Ipolyság, to finish rebaptizing it Šahy, had arrived in the morning; an order that wasn't one exactly, but rather a type of bureaucratic procedure without calculating the difficulties: "Forward ten kilometres!"

And after all, it was a spectacle, almost a fairy tale, that ended well for the good guys (the victors) and badly for the bad guys (the vanquished). Medium-sized cannons appeared in the palace courtyard, from who knows where. The soldiers tore down the wall that blocked their view of the city and, through the gap, adjusting the sight, pointed one of their cannons in its direction. And there, at the water's edge, on their horses, thirty or so Cossacks lined up holding two machine guns each, one under each arm, the controls in their mouths.

Until they stopped their rounds, until they halted, until a painful silence could be heard in which not even the horses changed their position. Total silence and stillness.

Five, ten minutes? No one could say. Perhaps it was no more than thirty seconds, or a minute at the most. Fenix's heartbeat, like his cousins', accelerated when, without hearing a single order called out first, they heard a *bang* and the cannons' mouths flashed, like a kind of echo; then a drum roll, and other roars coming from the other side of the path that led to the demolished bridges. The Cossacks spurred their horses and took off, overtaking the boats, which were heavier, despite the energy deployed by the rowers. The flash, the bang, the music from the cannons' mouths, didn't stop. The children watched, mesmerized, as the Cossacks' horses began to sink because of the water's high level. And beyond them, what was there?

Some say, and legend now has it, that many Cossacks who attacked from the other side, without forgetting the horses, were carried by the torrential flow of the water from the river that had flooded onto the fields. Others, that the Germans swatted them like flies. That more than a few boats sank. That the price the Russians paid was very high and that the seven or eight Germans that remained alive in the city square, around the Virgin, were gunned down, and met their end with their hands in the air; a futile sign of surrender to the Russians, unnecessary for them to be admitted into heaven or hell.

It was the last of the turmoil. The year of eating potatoes had passed but saying that normal life had returned—Fenix himself would say so—would be exaggerating. With a war, something dies in the soul—if not the soul itself—and is never recovered. However, the "Peaceful Days" returned, and with them—in spite of the broken windows, the demolished houses, the increased number of dead in the cemetery—life, or at least something that could be called a "simulation of life." Real life would be left for the future "Peaceful Days" during which, willingly or not, the memory of the horror that would only re-enter through the television screen would be lost.

The bridges were rebuilt. Given the lack of iron, and due to the urgency of needing to advance, wood was used. How they discovered the artisanal factory was a mystery. The Mistress affirmed that without a doubt someone envious of her fortune had betrayed her. What is certain is that the Russians weren't as kind as the neighbours who wanted to bury their dead and didn't ask her permission. The strongest beams and a few planks for the handrail made history: they would end up heating unknown homes when the final bridges were built.

The front had arrived, stayed some time and then went on its way. Cannon fire was heard again, including Stalin's Organ, but they were now familiar with this music; furthermore, the mouths of the cannons were pointing forward, toward the heads of others who were also waiting for the front. With the bridges rebuilt, other music came, that of the motors carrying the cannons and the tracks of the Russian tanks heading toward the front that, as they had already proven, did not bring joy. The children watched, amazed, and applauded the huge machines, bigger than the German ones. Yes, they were bigger, and instead of a swastika, they bore the hammer and sickle.

With the capture of the city and the arrival of the vehicles, the Russians—though not all of them—cleared out of the palace, and their convalescents (of whom, to tell the truth, there were few left) were brought elsewhere: those who had recovered went back to war; those who were crippled, with something missing, to their homes; and those who died were buried in unmarked graves.

Kultura.

The doctor who had greeted them didn't come, but rather his delegate, wearing his uniform and a white belt with a red cross on his arm; to speak, he removed his hat. Fenix translated: they had removed all the wounded, the cots, the instruments, they had put the paintings back up, the rugs back in their place and the family was allowed to re-occupy the house. He thanked them, said goodbye with a bow, put his hat back on and with another salute, a military one, disappeared. Since his mother didn't seem to want to give thanks, Fenix thanked them for her.

Curiously, one would think (any of them would swear it), that on the day when they could return, including his aunts and cousins to their homes, they would be jumping for joy. On the contrary; living underground had weighed heavily on them, in addition to the desire to return to living a normal life. In the instant that it was taken from them, they all felt an infinite weakness, so much so, that those who were standing sat, and those who were sitting on the mattresses on the floor, laid down. They had become accustomed to carrying this weight and it now seemed to them that an even greater one awaited them. Even his mother, who hadn't let a day go by without her reminding everyone of all the valuable things that there were in the palace, and who would burden them with her worry, sat and stayed silent for a long while. Maybe because she was the Mistress, even in front of her sisters and her father, she was the first to speak. After insulting the Russians, and the doctor, she said:

"Those damn crooks, on top of everything they broke, what did they steal?"

And, once more, silence and stillness.

It was not for nothing, Fenix believes, that God began his

Creation with light, separating it from darkness. Even during the day, including now that it was almost summer, they lived in a kind of half-darkness. The little window at the courtyard level didn't let in much light, apart from the door when, for a brief time, it was left open, including in the winter, to air out the basement. Thus, when the lone electric light bulb that hung from the ceiling in the middle of the basement was turned on, as though God were announcing the Creation or a poet, the Renaissance, the cry of jubilation was unanimous: civilization was returning, progress was returning, the little men inside the radio, who would continue lying as always (and they continue to lie to this day, although, today, still dwarves in soul and body, we see their faces on the screen) were returning.

The trumpet didn't sound but it was as though the morning bells were ringing. In the end, as though the weight had dissipated all at once, content, they stood up as though they had just finished a picnic—a long one, but a picnic all the same. His aunts and cousins, who had already consumed the provisions they had brought, gathered their belongings, and, leaving behind the mattresses made of flattened straw, began to leave. The grandfather offered his daughter help with the move, but the Mistress decreed that she would stay downstairs until there was not a single disgusting bloodstain left in the house. The grandfather, who had run out of wine and tobacco, now liberated, ran to the stable to unhitch his poor horse and go to his house to see if the winery had been saved, and to search for tobacco, somewhere, anywhere, even if it was in hell. The Mistress ordered Judit to deep clean the house. Now that there was light, they could surely fill the water tank without any issues. Judit looked at the light bulb and Fenix as well: it had gone out. He was going to inform his mother, who was standing in the doorframe, but Judit brought her index finger to her lips and shrugged her shoulders. At the moment when they climbed the stairs with the bucket and brush, Fenix looked at the light bulb again as it flickered; on, then off again. The electricity reminded him of something, but he didn't know what.

⇥ 11.

⅌——**WHEN THEY FINISHED** climbing the palace steps and opened the veranda doors, they noticed that a few of the lamps on the walls were lit. The light that had once again returned awakened in Fenix a memory that seemed vague and distant to him, charged with anxiety because of his inability to understand what it was. He was unaware of what would await him inside. Judit, on the other hand, with the brush in one hand and the bucket in the other, knew exactly what awaited her: slave labour.

Just as it had been announced, the sanatorium had disappeared. But the Russian army hadn't, or at least, not all of its constituents. When they entered the veranda (the light cut out once more), in addition to the slightly unpleasant odour (a mix of disinfectant, iodine and alcohol), they were struck by a chorus of laughter and loud voices. They were coming from the living room. They poked their heads in with caution: four or five officers were gathered around an object on the floor; one of them was kneeling. It wasn't difficult to see the bottle accompanied by a small cup circulating between them, and even less difficult for Fenix to guess and simultaneously deduce what was happening:

the officers were playing with his train that, probably, was stopping and going along with the power interruptions that he had seen in the light bulbs. And this is how it must have been happening: at this moment, silence, everyone watching what was going to happen; an "Oh!" and smiling faces could mean a Go, and the laughter, a Stop. Since Fenix knew nothing of courage or cowardice, without Judit having the time to hold him back, he ran into the room directly up to the officer who was kneeling and almost rolling onto the floor laughing. Yes, there was the train on its rails. While the officer that he knocked over stood back up, Fenix looked around. He couldn't see the box that it was kept in; he took a step forward and leaned over to pick up the locomotive and its wagons. And the rails? Disoriented, with the circle of officers closed around him, without knowing what to do as the wagons fell, on the verge of tears, with only the locomotive in his hand, he tried to make his escape by jumping over the kneeling officer, but the other one on his feet who blocked his path. Grumbling, kicking, he tried to go another way; useless, two officers joined together, more laughter, and passing through them was impossible. He ended up motionless, with the locomotive in one hand and making a fist with the other, rubbing his eyes full of tears.

Maybe the Kyrgyz didn't know that Russians adore children, but these, if they didn't adore them, they at least respected them and couldn't help but feel empathetic. Once their laughter had subsided, shaky, trembling cries in Slovak could be heard. "Leave … me alone! Let me go!" They all looked toward the door.

Judit had come in. A Cossack—the same one who had winked at her in the courtyard, Fenix was sure of it—more than a little drunk, with arms wide open, had trapped her against the wall and was mumbling things in her ear, or maybe trying to kiss her, since Judit desperately tried to fight him off with her elbows, shaking her head from side to side.

The officer who was on his knees, because of the size of his belly, stood up like a spring. With his right hand on his pistol, he took two steps and shouted something three times, so loud that he not only made the Cossack let go of Judit, but also paralyzed Fenix, who instantly stopped his wailing. The next orders were given in a softer voice, and the Cossack exited through the door and disappeared—perhaps swallowed by the earth, Fenix hoped.

The officer stopped next to Judit and told her:

"He is one of my assistants," he said. "Since the Germans killed his family, he's gone mad. Forgive him for this time. If he bothers you again, let me know and I will punish him. On top of that, he's a drinker." Then went quiet for a second. "No, it's not that, I drink too."

And he stood there with his head down, as though lost.

This time, the silence lasted a few seconds, until Fenix reacted and, with the locomotive, gaining momentum, preparing to jump toward Judit and the door. Just as he was about to launch himself forward, he was suddenly surrounded by the arms of the officer, who lifted him onto his belly and held him against his chest. He held him with one arm, and with the other, caressed his hair. Finally, after giving him a kiss on the forehead, he put him down onto the floor and with his hand on his little head, calmed him and asked him:

"Calm down, calm down, my son, nothing's going to happen to you. I'm not going to take your train, neither will the others, but, tell me, is it yours?"

Never in his life had poor Fenix been treated with so much affection by a man; a father who, without being asked to, did something more than mess his hair up: caressed him, gave him

a kiss, and now spoke to him in a booming voice that—the
ironies of life—calmed him, just as Judit's (now forgotten) lullabies made him sleep. With the joy of being recognized by a
man as a real, existing being, he remained silent, and managed
only to nod his head.

"Good. Now, as I told you, I won't take it from you, but I
would love to give it to my children. In Russia, we can't buy one.
I'll buy it off you, or, I should say, since money isn't worth anything anymore, nor do we even know which to use, I'll trade it
for whatever you want."

"Whatever you want" is quite a thing to say. In Fenix's mind,
there weren't many things to choose from or ask for. Without
realizing that this officer was treating him this way to trap him
with his kindness (on the other hand, he had all the power in
the world to take the train without explanation or justification), this man's affection won over his heart and with a smile,
an absolute innocence (or not so much; maybe he thought he
would win himself a father), pulled the locomotive away from
the chest and extended his hand to give it to the nice man.
Gently, the officer pushed it back up against Fenix's chest.

"What's your name?"

Fenix slurped up his mucus.

"Fenix Jacobowicz."

"A Polish family name? How strange! Well, anyway, that's
not my business. I'm Captain Vorosoff, and Captain Vorosoff
is a man of his word. I told you that you could ask me for whatever you want for it. That way you'll be satisfied and I'll have a
clear conscience. I'm listening."

The mystery of the quickness of the mind, accelerated or
halted by the unconscious. Fenix thought about it, but for no
more than twenty or thirty seconds, during which a few scenes
from children's stories ran through his mind, featuring horse-

men riding through forests of gold or silver, armed with spears and swords in search of dragons that devoured princesses, and although his mother wasn't one, a mere Mistress, if when the Kyrgyz tried to attack her she would have had a pistol—even a modest one, like the officer's—the whole ordeal would have unfolded very differently. Not to mention that damn Cossack that had been showboating in the courtyard, in front of Judit, winking at her, and now had tried to … tried to …

And he pointed to the holster on Captain Vorosoff's belt. After scratching the back of his neck, the Captain opened it and took out a Luger that he weighed in the palm of his hand.

"You know, Fenix, I stole this pistol from a German officer, whom I hope isn't resting in peace, after a battle in which I destroyed his … Well, the details aren't important but it's one of my most cherished memories. But, let me see. Put the locomotive in your other hand and give me your right one."

He did just that. His open hand barely fit into the centre of the Captain's palm. And although he had grown enough to become a man and have a secret lover, when Vorosoff put the butt of the pistol in his hand, saying "Close your hand," it barely covered half of the Luger's handle.

"Doesn't it seem a little big for you?"

He nodded, looking downcast.

"Wait," the Captain said.

He gave an order to what appeared to be a sub-officer, who went into the room that was once occupied by the German who was obsessed with the hygiene of the plant leaves and that now—Fenix would soon learn—would be occupied by the Captain for the next while. Two minutes later, he came out with a box that he handed to Vorosoff. Vorosoff went over to a small table, opened the box on top of it, and called Fenix over. Inside the box, wrapped in velvet, a variety of pistols, enough to defend, if not a nation, then at least a city. He took out a small one, shiny, chrome. He placed it in Fenix's hand. Fenix closed his fingers around it; it fit almost perfectly. Looking at the gun, happy, without even being fully conscious of its deadly effect, distracted, he handed the locomotive to the captain, who had to catch it quickly so it wouldn't fall on the floor. Still distracted, and in spite of what his maternal education had taught him through beatings, he forgot to say thank you, took a step toward the door, and again was caught by Vorosoff:

"Excuse me, could you give me the pistol for a few seconds?"

Fenix hesitated, but Vorosoff had already won his heart. He handed it over. The Captain took the cartridge, emptied the bullets, rotated the cylinder two or three times, looked down the barrel to check that it was empty, aimed toward the ground and pulled the trigger two or three times, put the cartridge back in and, holding it by the barrel, handed it back to him.

And with that, Fenix left the living room, running like a fool, pulling the trigger and shouting *bang bang* to replace the non-existent bullets. Yes, it was a form of defending his mother, or Judit if she were in danger, or the entire city with its golden trees, against any imaginable enemy, even against planes that drop bombs and kill people. The idea of showing the gun to his mother, to appease her and prove to her that he cared about her, to win her over, he took out of his mind with two or three imaginary slaps. As for his cousins, well, he would show them later. The gate was shut; he went out into the street by the side door; he ran, *bang bang*, to the first bridge over the lake, *bang bang*, put his foot on a plank that held the bannister in place and over the handrail, *bang bang*, cleared the horizon of enemies until he ran out of bullets and his soul, like the cartridge, was empty. And there he stood, holding the handrail, staring at the water of the lake, conjuring the image of he and Judit skating.

Something wasn't right; a cloud descended from the sky, or a mist rose from the lake, or maybe it was nothing more than fog, a fog in which the past was buried but had now returned to try to tell its story, or worse, explain itself.

Whether true or not, he felt that he had betrayed Judit, that he had sold her for thirty miserable pieces of silver, had given up the locomotive that had brought him a new happiness he had never felt before, a locomotive that could have brought him even further; *no, no, no,* he told himself, it can't be—or he says it to himself now. And after all, did he really want to save his mother, when so many times he had felt the desire to kill her? Yes, he felt it, he lived it, it hurt him and disturbed him just as much, until … until he couldn't bear it any longer and, with the pistol in his hand, he wound his arm back and with a strong thrust …

Maybe it was violent because of his rage and fury: the pistol traced a curve and, when it hit the water with a *splash* and sank with a *blub*, Fenix felt that something had been liberated inside of him, something that was rising and that he would carry with him. It wasn't very far, no. It didn't levitate. It was more that, whether he wanted it or not, a small burden was left with him, a subtle punishment for the sin of betrayal that, every now and then, would manifest throughout his life as a knot in his stomach. Or would it be from one of the other sins or betrayals that he would accumulate? It wouldn't matter. A good shot of rum would undo it.

⚡ 12.

᪥——**FENIX BOLTED BACK** to the palace. He saw lamps lit in the veranda. In the living room, he didn't see anyone. Through the sliding door that expanded it and gave way to the bedroom that was once the German's and now Vorosoff's, he heard his booming voice as well as the other officials. It is true that Vorosoff hadn't asked for permission to settle in there (just like the German), but it is also certain that even though he didn't show his love for humanity by cleaning the leaves of some of the plants that were left alive, he never opened the sliding door, and exited instead through the door that led to the courtyard. Including when he was just visiting, which rarely occurred, he would go through there, and knock on the door to the living room, or ask permission if it was open.

Fenix looked at the room; the paintings were back in their places, same as the rugs. But, on the piano, the hammer and sickle with the inscription underneath were still there, and would remain there for a long time. They would be there until fifty years later when Fenix would return from America to look for the treasures hidden by his mother. However, between the rugs, absorbed by the wood of the parquet flooring, and although due to their dark colour, they could well have passed for some other stain or flaw in the wood (if Fenix knew it, then his mother must have been more than aware, along with the entire city) these stains were blood—even worse, human blood—and since they were "disgusting," his mother wished to eliminate them.

But where was Judit? With a certain feeling of uneasiness, without a train to bring him nor the locomotive to guide him, he began to search for her. He found her in the master bedroom, on her knees, scrubbing the floor with a soapy boar bristle brush. Fenix was going to surprise her by covering her eyes from behind but the presence of another woman wearing a kerchief on her head, an apron, old clothes and who, with a rag in her hand, was cleaning the window, stopped him. Fenix had never seen her before, and observed her; she looked like a painter in front of a canvas, on which she was giving the finishing touches, but with a rag instead of a paintbrush; a touch over here and she took a step back to look at the result; another other there, a step back. Between surprise and curiosity, he stood there observing her until he heard an "Oof!" and Judit's voice:

"It's useless, Madam, the stains won't come out."

The woman at the window turned around; from her face and the look of annoyance, Fenix recognized his mother. The Mistress, who had disguised herself as a servant, approached Judit.

"I'm sure you're doing it wrong!"

And with her fists on her hip, lightly bent over, she scrutinized the floor.

"Please, Madam, watch me do it, tell me if it isn't right, or how I should do it."

"Brush hard!"

Judit wet the brush in the bucket, passed some soap over the floor and brushed.

"Harder!"

She did.

"Harder, harder!"

Judit, with a sigh, sat up on her heels, wiped the back of her hand across her forehead and said:

"I'm sorry, Mistress, I can't do it any harder. It just won't come out ..."

"Move! You're useless!"

And the Mistress herself got on her knees to brush with all the vigour and strength that her size allowed, which was not insignificant. Fenix and Judit watched: the stain remained the same. The Mistress was merciless with it. Nothing. Judit commented:

"Do you see what I mean, Madam?"

The Mistress became infuriated. She threw the brush into the bucket and barked:

"Get out of here, both of you!"

If Fenix is remembering properly, they were the first words his mother addressed to him as a greeting that day.

That day, with "disgusting stains" or not, after a hectic ordeal of infernal cleaning that the Mistress invited both her sisters to participate in ("You look like you're trying to clean your original sin! Maybe you weren't baptized?" one of them said to her; a comment that didn't receive a response), that day, they moved back into the palace.

Once night fell, dinner didn't have major variations from the lunches and dinners in the basement. Instead of stews, baked potatoes with butter that the grandfather brought over along with two bottles of wine. His winery had remained intact thanks to a rickety cupboard that he had used to hide the entrance. He was still smoking corn silk instead of tobacco.

That night, after dinner (he doesn't remember when it was,

not even the year; only that summer was near), Fenix managed his first triumph—and maybe the only one for many years—over his mother. Although there were many spare rooms, including a laundry room and a room for ironing, there was no maid's chamber in the palace. Since Judit's house was still in ruins, the Mistress wanted to establish a service unit by ordering Judit to sleep in the basement. Fenix objected:

"No, I don't want her to sleep there."

"Whether you want it or not, little friend, it's me who decides," his mother declared, like an authentic Mistress.

Despite the danger it implied, Fenix threw a fit.

"You *decided* that she would take care of me. I want her to sleep here. Outside there are soldiers and they're bad."

"I have the right to change my mind anytime I want. There will be no further discussion."

More than a few crystal and porcelain pieces that were kept in the bathroom were broken. His mother hadn't stopped watering them with her tears, but this did not provoke the miracle of uniting the broken pieces. They hadn't taken them all out but some pieces had gone back to decorate the living room, among them a French or Chinese vase (who could remember?) whose price his mother had announced like the sound of a trumpet at the moment when she placed it on a column near the Russian stove, in a very visible place. And it was to this column that Fenix, lamenting having thrown the revolver in the lake, ran and picked up the vase:

"If she doesn't stay, I'll break it."

His mother took a step.

"If you come any closer, I'll break it."

His mother stopped dead; from between her teeth that she was grinding, a fierce insult came out that made reference to herself. It ended with:

"Just like your father. Or worse, a little ..."

If it was an accident caused by his nervous trembling over this confrontation with his mother, or if he did it on purpose, makes no difference. What is certain is that the vase seemed to slip from his hands; his mother shrieked.

"OK, you win, this time you've won. But the price will be high, very, very high. Go get washed up. You smell like a pig."

That night, in the absence of a maid's chamber, Judit, who had sweat from the excessive work, washed herself as much as she could in an auxiliary bathroom and prepared her bed on a sofa in a room adjacent to Fenix's in which his scattered toys could be found, the majority of which were brought home by his father, and whose existence had now been forgotten. And much more than these had been forgotten, which, out of spite, out of vengeance, out of rage, he had furtively put into the Russian stove, where they burned with the dignity of the wood.

The sofa wasn't very big. When Judit, after reading Fenix a story, tucking him in, and waiting for him to fall asleep, laid down on the couch, she needed to bend a little to fit. She was waiting for, and yet, was surprised when Fenix laid down in the hollow formed by her body. He fit perfectly. They intertwined their naked legs, Judit lifted her thighs a little to shelter him with warmth and protection. And solace; perhaps because of his rebellion against his mother, waves of shudders ran through Fenix.

There were no games that night. Tired, they both fell asleep almost instantly; through their skin, safe together, two souls made one, they floated in space like in a fairy tale, up to the stars.

Fenix, hugging a pillow in which he could smell the absent presence of Judit, woke up in his own bed. Yes, he knew that Judit, under the Mistress's orders, would already be scrubbing the floor or removing the already cleaned, non-existent dust that floated in his mother's mind. Calling for Judit would be useless. He hugged the pillow harder, buried his face in it and remained that way, snoozing, dreaming, imagining, remembering, until in his mind the image of Vorosoff resurged, with whom, whether he wanted it or not, things weren't clear at all. On one hand, he resented him for having taken his train, especially the precious locomotive. Well, taken or not, traded for something as useless as a gun, and especially now that the "Peaceful Days" seemed to have returned. Restless, without having a clear understanding that he was still bothered, with the vague idea of getting the train back somehow, he hopped out of bed, got dressed, and this time, tied his shoes. In seconds, he was already outside.

On the veranda, he could see Captain Vorosoff wrapped in a cloak, wearing a cap, surrounded by officers. It wasn't the perfect moment to address the issue. But the Captain saw him and, from Fenix's face, guessed what was happening inside him, took a hand out from the cloak, signalled to him to approach, a signal that he emphasized with his loud booming voice:

"Come over here!"

Partially forgetting the motives for his own presence, he ran up to him.

"I've already sent the train to Russia, for my children," the Captain said.

Upon seeing the transformation in Fenix's face, Vorosoff caressed his head and told him:

"You know what? I put a letter in the package, telling them that you were the one sending it to them, a nice boy, very generous, with a big heart."

He gave a sigh (all things considered, he wasn't as bad as his mother said) that signalled a profound relief in Fenix, who looked at the Captain with a smile that mirrored the smiles of the other officers, including Vorosoff, who believed that the child was accepting the loss, and not that the sigh was proof of his existence and a confirmation of his value as a human being. However, once seeded, doubt is eternal.

"Is that true?" Fenix asked him.

"The most absolute truth. And now I must go. I have lots of work to do. I'm the general commander of this front and in charge of the city. On that note, do you know how to play chess?"

"No."

"Alright then. If I come back early tonight, I'll teach you. Alright?"

Although he had cousins to play with, Vorosoff's offer meant gaining another friend. A kind of older brother, too.

"Alright!" he exclaimed, with so much enthusiasm that the officers started laughing.

The door opened, and Vorosoff went out, with the other officers following behind. Fenix watched how, as they descended the stairs, their heads disappeared one by one. Once he was outside, a car wasn't waiting for the captain as one did for the German officer: he climbed into a half-track that looked a little worse for wear, in which the other officers barely fit. Fenix followed the vehicle into the street. Ah, this, however, the German officer didn't have: a tank that, no less worn than the half-track, hitched behind it, an escort fit for a general (or in the Russians' case, a marshal).

At night, with mixed feelings, out of love or an unspeakable desire for some form of vengeance resurfacing, Fenix waited for the Captain to no avail to play chess. He had taken it for granted in spite of his "if I come back early." The little one couldn't know that the bombs didn't destroy the bar that his father frequented and that it was likely that, for Vorosoff, the bar had been a discovery where he would make up for the basic necessities he was lacking that confirmed his status as a man and would make him a better commander. In that regard, Fenix had no reason to envy him; noting his bitterness, that night Judit held him between her thighs, his nest, with more warmth than ever.

The electricity that powered the house and the radio finally stopped cutting out. The little men kept announcing Hitler's imminent triumph, as soon as the secret weapons would enter into action, but now, with so many false promises on both sides, including the triumph of the Allies that was just as imminent, exhausted, there were few left who believed any of the news anymore, and many lost interest. It was more important to obtain a little meat protein to eat with the potatoes, bread or glasses of milk. The grandfather, with the horse that he had managed to save thanks to his thinness and the carriage that had saved itself, returned to live in his house at the foot of the Calvary, with his base of operations, the winery, within reach. He resumed his trade of selling the wine that had saved itself from all the thirsts, and travelled through the surrounding areas and the little nearby towns. Thanks to the peasants who took better care of their animals than they did their wives, or to the war that hadn't fully passed, he would supply the palace with eggs, chickens, geese, flour at a cost so high that Fenix's mother, suspicious of her own father, felt dizzy every time she finished paying, and would need to take a seat in an armchair. This amused the grandfather, who was making a killing, and his pipe, now full of real tobacco, would spill out little clouds of smoke as though it were laughing along with him. A few Jews returned—very few—but Fenix's friend, whom he would never forget, did not figure among them.

And the only member of the family who was missing returned at last: his father. One more surprise in Fenix's soul: Fenix didn't realize that, despite the fact that he paid more attention to his reflection in the mirror than his own son, he loved him so much: upon seeing him appear in the living room, a burst of adoration surged from him like a volcano erupting from his soul, and with a cry that was the complete opposite of the one he'd let out when he attacked the Kyrgyz, he jumped on him with such force that they both fell to the floor; and there, frantic, he hugged him and waited for it to be reciprocated, which would have compensated for all the affection he had never received, and confirmed his existence like a second birth, a second baptism. But it didn't come this time, either.

His father, accustomed to other kinds of caresses, felt uncomfortable and struggled to his feet. Fenix noticed and anticipated it quickly, as though spontaneous: he stretched out his hand to help him get up, and with the same speed and spontaneity, hid his hand behind his back to join it with the one that was already there and, feeling more than a little embarrassed for him, as well as for himself for having helped him, stood there staring at him, noticing that he was a little fatter than he remembered. With an uncomfortable smile, his father, as though he were in front of the mirror, began to shake off the hypothetical dust that Judit's meticulous cleaning would have left behind on the rug. The discomfort in his smile intensified when he realized that he was being watched by his wife, Judit, the grandfather and his son down whose cheeks rolled two, three silent tears. Many years later, many, too many, Fenix would understand that a person who is deprived of affection cannot learn to give it themselves. Yes, he would understand this, would even reconcile with it, but, against his own will, wouldn't, nor did he even know, how to forgive him. However, something positive would come of it: the guilt he felt toward his father would be minor compared to the guilt he felt toward his mother. At least he never struck him even once in his life, instead opting for a more humane way of ignoring him. Clearly, he would do one or two worse things, but that is life.

The first to speak was the Mistress, who welcomed him:

"Hello. Have you finished cleaning yourself yet or should I get Judit to bring a brush?"

"Welcome, Sir," Judit greeted him, curtsying like a ballerina, putting the tip of one foot behind the heel of the other and bending her knee with a bow.

"Hello, my son-in-law. I see that the battle you fought didn't dirty your clothes."

"Fight, this one? I'm sure he cleaned under the bed before he hid under there, in his hometown."

His father roared with laughter that was a little forced, finishing with:

"Well, after that fabulous welcome, all that's left for me to do is leave."

The grandfather smiled.

"Don't be silly. You know we're teasing. There's wine, we're going to celebrate your return. Or maybe you'd like to eat first?"

"I can wait. First let's toast. From my hometown I brought an exceptional *pálinka* and two or so kilos of *kolbász*, since I figured we'd be lacking food around here. I'm going to get my suitcase."

"Go on then. I can tell from your chubby cheeks that fighting a war isn't tiring work."

During this very loving welcome, Judit noticed Fenix's sadness. She approached him, took him by the shoulder and drew him toward her. He sought shelter by putting a leg between hers, his face between her breasts and his arms around her waist. Judit, with a hand on the back of his neck and the other on his head, caressed him gently.

Before going out, Fenix's father stopped to look at them and exclaimed: "Look how much that boy has grown!" as if he weren't referring to his own son.

Judit caught his attention. If Fenix had grown, Judit had matured no less, going from a slightly chubby girl to a real grown woman. Her waist was well defined, and even more so with Fenix's hug. Her breasts, still without a girdle, seemed to want to move forward from her chest with a type of involuntary defiance; her face had become more angular and her features stood out from the frame of her long flowing hair, which she sometimes tied with a buckle and a kerchief when she needed to work.

The Master of the palace had no interest in staff hierarchy. Only years later, remembering it—not exactly, obviously—he would understand the meaning of his mother's comment:

"So it's come to this. I'd like to inform you that the bar is still open, or has reopened its doors. Mind you, you'll be mixed up with several Russian officers, but I believe that they wash and perfume themselves nicely in order to impress young women less innocent than the one you're looking at." She finished with a warning: "Don't even think about it, let alone try it. Fenix would stab you."

His grandfather had already gone out to get the wine. His father slipped out to fetch his suitcase.

≶ 13.

※——**A BRIEF RECAP:** there was practically nothing left of Fenix's father's artisanal factory. The Germans, as though they were provisions in times of war, had taken all things metal for themselves, the machines with their motors included; the Russians exhausted the stock of wood, mainly the thickest pieces to build the bridges, and the few planks that were left over were taken to make caskets to bury the dead officers; the artisanal products of the warehouse, from cutting boards and wooden spoons to salad bowls, could still be found decades later in many of the nice neighbours' houses. With the exception of one or two cans of thinner, many cans of paint and varnish disappeared to decorate furniture elsewhere, and twenty-four or twenty-five Russians took charge of the cans of thinner and threw a party when they discovered them. It isn't known exactly how many they were, but it was very easy to count those who died of intoxication, and whose eyes searched for the beginning of the path to the great voyage: seventeen.

As owner, Fenix's father was accused of poisoning them and ended up at the police station, controlled at the time by the NKVD who set the common criminals free and instead filled it with politicians. Fenix remembers that that first time, it was no more than two or three days, during which, accompanied by Judit, he would bring him lunch. Once it was proven that there was no intentionality, and that the dead soldiers acted of their own volition, they freed him, only to bring him in again a week later, this time accusing him of other crimes. The first, of being rich, not to mention the owner of a factory that exploited its poor workers; the second, of having hidden an English secret agent before the arrival of the Germans and having brought him with him to who knows where. And although his father argued that he had brought him to his destination, as he had been commanded by the Communist Party of which he was a member, and that in those days the English were allies, he remained incommunicado and it wasn't known if the food that his son— now alone—brought him every day ever reached his mouth.

When he was released a month later, he told his son that it did reach him, but only in part. He looked more dead than alive. He had spent a week in solitary confinement and although he wasn't beaten, he suffered endless, more subtle torture methods, of a psychological nature. Once it was confirmed that, with regard to the Englishman, he had acted according to the Party's orders, he was absolved, but he still wasn't released. Explain to us, Comrade, how is it that a real communist could own a factory and exploit workers? A kind of tribunal, now civil, had been formed, composed of honourable members of the Party, before which all the workers and employees of the artisanal factory presented themselves, or at least those who hadn't been wiped out by the war or who didn't escape to better worlds and who, thank God, weren't many, and now quite old and full of kindness. Whether it was the truth, or just luck, no one denounced his father. On the contrary, they praised him for his generosity, his concern for the workers' well-being, including their families. The Mistress commented: "You have no idea that charity begins at home and you consider the workers as integral parts of a court you never had." From this month of prison, if Fenix isn't remembering incorrectly, was born the first of his catchphrases, a demonstration of his intelligence and not of his affection, which would continue to serve him throughout his life, especially in his adolescence in Argentina. And he heard his father say it in the living room, now a Lord once again, smoking fake Coronas and drinking *pálinka* instead of whiskey, sitting in an armchair, waiting for dinner to be served on the dining room table that the white, immaculate table cloth had returned to. He told him: "The best part of a revolution, my son, the most beautiful, illusory, is doing it; afterward, all that is left to do is go elsewhere to start a new one."

They would all move elsewhere, but his father wouldn't start a new revolution, if he had even participated in the one that was ongoing.

With the looting of his artisanal factory, the banks closed, the money lost, with no savings to speak of (although the Mistress was an expert at accumulating gold and hiding it away), the noble Jacobowicz remained at a standstill, with no prospect of recovering. At the time, Fenix knew very little of the family secrets that parents hide, although sometimes they let them out in front of the children, counting on the innocence and incomprehension that comes with their age, but forgetting that the little ones have memories. It was at this time, and in this situation, Fenix heard the first whisper of a life that occurred before he existed (or, he guesses, before the Mistress, against her will, began carrying him in her belly). He was, as his mother reminded him, among those who shouldn't have been born. The aristocrat Jacobowicz, finding himself in a desperate situation, in order to begin his life again in some way, or continue to live the way he had before, appealed to his deserving wife who, as Lady of the house, with her farm, had obtained more cash than the priest of a rich parish and, facing the general insecurity, had been converting it into the vile metal known as gold. No one knew how much, but her husband was sure that she had it—but where she had hidden it, not even the devil knew. Upon his plea for help, this was, more or less, the answer Fenix overheard:

"You've already taken everything from me, and in a filthy way, by making me marry you. Now, that's enough. Sort it out on your own. Maybe your little whores at the bar can help you."

"Probably more than you. Those women you call whores tend to have a good heart."

But the nobleman didn't even have the money to go get a drink at the bar and see if they would help him—which would certainly have been doubtful, anyway. It wasn't clear either, in spite of having been freed from prison clean of all guilt, why the Communist Party didn't help him. Years later, he would say that from the way they had treated and tortured him (in his case, nothing serious, something along the lines of crumpling his suit or asking him too many questions), he had already begun to distance himself from that ideal and the desire to cut ties stopped him (morally, he would emphasize) from asking the Party for money. Fenix now suspects, after piecing it together over the years, that the Party followed without being very sure about him and kept him in a kind of quarantine. Indeed, there was one form of help available to him, which he rejected: working as a foreman in a furniture factory. According to his mother's version: "A big man like him couldn't lower himself to work under someone else." According to his father's, he wasn't made to be a policeman and an informant who would denounce those who were suspected to be counterrevolutionaries.

On the topic of versions, his father had no shortage of

them. He would speak at length about the indignity of being a merchant since it requires no creativity and to substantiate his disdain, he would cite Montesquieu: "All is lost when the *lucrative* profession of the merchant becomes an *honourable* position." Even if in this case it could be the same, when Fenix would later come across the quote while casually reading, he would realize that his father had replaced the word "financier" with "merchant," another suspicion or almost certainty would arise: if his father had been a financier and in the end hadn't failed as a merchant, would he have spoken in the same way? Maybe so, as is the case with a cynical millionaire. And, the ironies of life, still in a somewhat communist Czechoslovakia, his father would begin his career as a "pure" merchant thanks to a self-professed natural-born communist who was certain that soon the entire world would be: the city's commander.

At this stage of this story he is remembering, the little city was completely occupied. The front was already far away and Captain Vorosoff, in his commandeering quality, had already lifted the curfew, but not the blackout order during the night. Not so much for the fear that the Germans would come back and strike, as for the fear that some enthusiastic squadron of allied planes—an American one, for example—that had left-over bombs and needed to use them, would release them, be it for some practice exercise, or simply for the sake of it. Vorosoff always had two assistants with him: there was the educated one who always carried a voluminous folder and, every time the captain would ask him a question or give an order, would open and consult it; the other was the little Cossack who, in addition to his job as an assistant, had two other purposes in his life: getting drunk, and throwing himself at Judit every time he saw her. While his style varied with his blood-alcohol level, the result was always the same, as with the feelings of jealousy in

Fenix (sometimes he had the impression that Judit wasn't bothered by him, and that she would only slip away if he was too drunk) and his feelings of hate.

With the city pacified, to put it one way, Captain Vorosoff, with the exception of one or two nights when he would stay at the bar, became a "homebody". In the morning he would get into the half-track with his two assistants, escorted by the tank, and would return at dusk. Sometimes he would ask Judit nicely to prepare dinner for him, which he ate alone in his bedroom; others, if he had visitors, always officers, he would bring his dinner and ask only for it to be reheated, which was done by Judit or by his assistant with the folder, who also often served him. At that time, the Cossack would already have disappeared; completely drunk, with other Cossacks, snoring away in the basement that was once the refuge of the Jacobowicz family and their relatives.

With Fenix's father cleared of all charges, Vorosoff, as though during his incarceration he hadn't known what was happening with him, began to regularly visit his hosts. When he ate alone, once his dinner was finished, he would down his last shot of vodka, the only thing he drank (he had politely declined the wine that the grandfather tried to sell or offer him); he would go through the veranda to get to the living room door and gently knock, the nobleman would open it and point to the little table on which the chessboard was already prepared. They would each sit in a chair; to the left of the board, a bottle of plum *pálinka* (the only deviation from the path of vodka that Vorosoff would allow himself) with two little glasses. Fenix's father would serve, and they would toast to Stalin, the end of the war, Vorosoff's return home and a great future Communist world. As though to make himself more comfortable, Vorosoff would undo his belt, take the Luger out from the holster and place it on the little table, to the right of the board. And they would begin to play: while the Luger was there, and even more so when Vorosoff's king was threatened and he would put his index on the trigger guard and make the pistol slowly spin on the table, Fenix's father would invariably lose.

Once or twice, he had the opportunity to win, which he owes to his son. The Luger, despite the association with the pistol Fenix sold his soul for, and the rift it had caused between him and Vorosoff, who didn't nurture the affection he had awakened in him (with the excuse that he was busy, he didn't fulfill his promise to teach him to play chess), attracted him like something authentic, that would actually fire, unlike the remnants of war with which they played in the field and which they could never get to work no matter how hard they tried. Many times he would stop beside the little table to watch the game; his father, concentrating on the board in order not to win, wouldn't even notice; Vorosoff, confident in his superiority, knowing that he would win, every now and then would look at him and smile, and even give him little taps on the shoulder to get back to the game. And one day, an impulse or inspiration, made him do what the Captain did: put his index finger on the trigger guard and make the Luger spin. Vorosoff's smile widened. He took the Luger, and with a few manoeuvres, did the same as with the other revolver: emptied it and put it in his little palm, which didn't cover much more surface area than the first time he tried it. And while *bang bang*, he ran through the palace killing enemies, his father gave himself the luxury, or rather, he dared to win against Vorosoff, whose face Fenix didn't find very smiley when he returned to the table and gave back the gun with a "Thank you." Vorosoff loaded it again, put it back in the holster, and, that night, he didn't feel like playing anymore.

Before saying goodbye, two glasses of *pálinka*, and maybe a bit more vodka in his bedroom, would console him.

With time, Captain Vorosoff began to change. He seemed increasingly drunk but in reality he was feeling more comfortable, more relaxed with the Jacobowicz, a kind of second family—an artificial one, but family all the same. By order or suggestion, the Mistress (who couldn't stand Vorosoff, or rather couldn't stand anyone who was in her territory against her will), through Judit or Fenix, would have dough and a dessert more succulent when the "Peaceful Days" returned with more intensity and walnuts and hazelnuts were obtained in abundance.

Thus, between games, chewing on the cakes, Vorosoff would tell them more about his life back in Russia, just as he became more interested in theirs. He had been born in the country and joined the military at a very young age. And in the military, although he had studied, he spent his entire career and became a captain not through the academies, where young men from good families even learned to dance, but through his own merits during the war. He had been awarded various medals for his valour and was even invited to join the Communist Party, which he accepted. The only thing he was missing, he said, was the Lenin medal. He didn't consider himself a man of good taste or bad taste (philosophical concepts, to him), but it seemed very strange to him that a human being should have places in his house where he defecates, which to him seemed almost like doing it on the table. He had prohibited all his men from using the palace bathrooms with their toilets and had had an outhouse built at the back of the garden that the soldiers used as a bathroom.

"And you, Captain?" Fenix's father asked.

"Well, I suffer quite a bit. I bathe in the bar hotel, but for hierarchical reasons, I can't go where my soldiers go and I have

to wait to reach the offices of the city, where it's more under-
standable to have indoor bathrooms. When I'm only going to
urinate, I use a chamber pot and in the morning I throw it all
out the window."

Although he knew that Fenix's father was a member of the
party, he never asked him why he was incarcerated, but he listened attentively to the financial problems that burdened him.
And one day, after having heard a kind of final complaint, that
Fenix's father, apart from his wedding ring, had nothing left to
sell and that, taking advantage of the situation that the war had
brought, people didn't pay very well, Vorosoff stayed silent and
remained that way for a while as he scratched the back of his
neck and, as though he were inspecting the room, looked out
the window up at the cloudless sky, then stared at the walls and,
with a sip of *pálinka* followed by a snort, finished the inspection.

Fenix will never be able to forget the way that Vorosoff
would get up from his seat. It was as though with a slight bend
he let his gut fall and, drawn by gravity, it tended toward the
floor and he, to stop it from reaching there, would stand up.
That night there was no variation of the form, but there was of
the substance; at the last moment he remembered the Luger
that he had put in its holster and, taking a step toward the door,
he told his father to follow him. And since he didn't explicitly
tell Fenix not to, he lined up behind him.

Since Vorosoff had occupied it, Fenix had never entered
into the ample bedroom and did so now as though he were
entering Ali Baba's cave, just like in Judit's stories. He dares to
say today that his father was bewildered, even green with envy;
in his palace, there was a room that contained objects more
valuable than in any of the others, but these were not his property. The floor was covered by a handmade Persian rug that

had probably come from a castle, so big that to extend it fully it needed to be trimmed to fit around the stove. Maybe he didn't know, but Vorosoff, by accident, had invented the moquette. In the middle of the bedroom, surrounded by chairs upholstered with silk, a table in the style of one of the Louis, lined with wood of different colours, including golden, that had never been there before. Not to mention the velvet armchairs and the curtains of the same material, or the trunk in one corner, the kind that pirates hide their treasures in. In this moment they understood why Vorosoff didn't use the double sliding door: a kind of cupboard, combination of a chest of drawers with a mirror in a golden frame like a painting full of crystals, vases and, in the middle, a beautiful samovar, the first Fenix had ever seen in his life. Next to it, on a silver tray, a bottle of vodka and several glasses. He opened one of the doors and took out a pitcher made of bronze. He called the father and told him to put his hands together and hollow his palms. Vorosoff picked up the pitcher, leaned it forward and poured out hundreds, maybe thousands of lighter stones. Fenix's father didn't know what to do. Vorosoff laughed and said:

"With this you can start a business—not very worthy of a communist, but you need to live and feed your son somehow."

After giving Fenix the order of going ahead to open the doors for him, his father, with his palms stuck together, exited through the one Vorosoff used and it closed with the sound of a wise ogre's laughter behind it. Fenix would never forget them, and as the years passed, he would become certain that the peasant Vorosoff had seen right through his father.

And this was how, with a fist full of goods rarer than the chickens that were brought from places the army hadn't gone through, his father started his business, first in sales, then purchasing North American cigarettes, contraband to rebuild his fortune as a good communist, a fortune that, although part of it would be absorbed by the bar, one day would bring them to Argentina.

After the episode at his father's factory when the soldiers drank paint thinner, Fenix knew that that was no exception, that the Russian soldiers, to get drunk, would drink everything they could find that had even a faint smell of alcohol. The soldiers had their ration of vodka (legend has it, Stalingrad, or the ruins of Stalingrad, were saved thanks to the barrels that rolled up to its defenders), but those who conquered the little city either didn't receive it in time or didn't receive it at all; and they need-ed to live. Anything was enough to stimulate the blood: at-tacking to rid themselves of their fury, numbing themselves, blinding themselves, losing their senses, forgetting. Fenix always compares the present to the past or speaks of history: in this case he could point to the desperate need for drugs of the young people of today and that, with a label hanging from their big toe, end up in the morgue, a place more elegant than out in the open air or in an unmarked grave. Ultimately, anyone who ab-sorbed Argentinian culture is one to talk; what about the bottles of rum that he empties to calm himself, and the Cuban cigars he smokes for stimulation?

He remembers that it was a Saturday or a Sunday, but he isn't sure. He can only suppose, because it was around noon and Vorosoff was in his bedroom; he believes that he was still sleep-ing off the previous night's bender at the bar. His assistants were wandering freely; on the veranda, the one with the folder, the more respectful one, was cleaning the captain's boots. He heard screams, and had no doubt they were coming from his mother. He crossed the living room and at that moment, coming out of the bedroom, behind his mother who was howling but without daring to touch it, the young Cossack, with a square-shaped bottle in his hand, staggering. "My Chanel! My Chanel number 5!" his mother was shrieking. And the young Cossack brought the bottle to his lips, finished emptying it and, with a wide and somewhat idiotic smile, handed it to his mother with a "Thank you" in Russian. His mother, still screaming, went up to Fenix as though he were to blame, just as he was for all his father's sins. And punished as well.

"Look what you—I mean, what he— has done!" and she shook the empty bottle in front of Fenix's nose. "He drank all of my perfumes. All of them! And with how much they cost me!"

Fenix was terrified. Not even today does he understand why: if it was the fear of being beaten or slapped by his mother, or because of the obnoxious young Cossack, who, still staggering, with one hand, pulled his sabre out halfway and then put it back into its sheath. What is certain is that Judit, taking refuge behind his mother (this is why she didn't see her), jumped beside her and, with a look of relief, put her hands on her shoulders. The young Cossack, as soon as he saw her, threw himself at her. Judit didn't know what to do; she hesitated between leaving him to escape and protecting him. They could have escaped, the two of them together, but they didn't have the time, and the young Cossack, with an insolence that no one had ever dared to show, hugged her and struggled to make her fall to the floor, which he managed to do. His mother, paralyzed, couldn't ask for help or scream as she did for her perfumes if the possibility had occurred to her. In Fenix, in spite of the memory of the Kyrgyz or because of it, the terror disappeared and gave way to jealousy and hate (he couldn't know that it would hurt so much) made his foot catapult forward and, since the young Cossack was half on Judit and half on the floor with his knees apart, that was where he kicked and the echo could be heard: a howl of pain brought him to his feet with a roar of rage.

It was not for nothing that he was a Cossack, and not for nothing that he carried a sabre; with his left hand, he snatched the sheath and with the right squeezed his fist tight, the graze of metal against metal could be heard and the sabre flailed into the air and there it stayed, flailing, while Judit had already gotten back onto her feet and jumped in front of Fenix to cover him. Clinging to her hip, he watched as the young Cossack, slowly, very slowly, shook his head and, surprised, observed the consequences of his so resolute and energetic act. His mother brought her hands to her head and cried out: "The horror!" She made her escape to call for help. He understood: unless it was chickens, geese, ducks, or the pig they would kill every year, she couldn't stand the sight of blood. Judit exclaimed: "My God!" and covered her mouth to stifle other exclamations.

The stillness of the young Cossack was absolute; he only looked at the puddle of blood that was forming under his hand that held the sheath, as though searching for its origin, which Judit and Fenix could see all too well: when he pulled out the sword, it became clear that he had cut two fingers so deeply that not only were they bleeding; they seemed to be hanging by a mere thread.

Not even today can Fenix imagine what was going through his mind, hazy from the toxic vapours of the perfume. What he will never forget is that he acted as though he were sleepwalking, or like a child: with his shoulder still raised, he dropped the sheath and extended the hand with the two hanging fingers, as though it were an offering. Judit, desperate, didn't know what to do. Fenix ran out to look for help while Judit ran into the kitchen for clean napkins and a floor mop (ah, the ghostly influence of the Mistress). By the time Fenix came back with the other assistant, the sword was back in its sheath, the hand had been wrapped by the Cossack himself, but the other, not the one that continued to bleed, now in awe, as though in a trance, could not understand what had happened to him. Upon seeing him, without entering, the insult that the assistant with the folder threw at him was familiar to them. He left and a few minutes later reappeared with two soldiers who grabbed the young Cossack, not very gently. Judit continued cleaning up the blood and Fenix followed them to the veranda door. Before it closed, he heard the word "hospital."

—⌇ 14.

⌇—THE SINISTER FREEDOM THAT had settled in on the day of the first bombing continued to reign, and even expanded. The parents, busy rebuilding their lives or embroiled in dark vengeance (some racist, Hungarians versus Slovaks who now, after the re-conquest, were Czechoslovaks), contributed significantly. Summer had arrived; the river had returned to its bed until the next thaw, and in the fields fertilized by the water, the first haystacks began to pile up, which would feed the few cows that were left and that must have spent the war in beds while the peasants slept in the stables, because despite their disdain for the nobility, because of the need to fight and confront that disdain, the peasants were cunning; if not, how could they have supplied the city?

With this freedom, Fenix, with his cousins and other children, would wander through the fields and forests. And the world was astonishing. They had never imagined that the war would be so vast and foreign. Despite their occasional outings, they had reduced it to the basement where they sheltered themselves from the bombs and cannon fire. Yes, they had witnessed the city's occupation. During the winter, when they would go skating, the four or five bombs that they wanted to detonate ended up being nonsense compared to the equipment they now had at their disposal. They had never imagined that the war would span practically the entire surface of the earth, as far as it could possibly reach. Unlike the children of today, who need to make an enormous mental effort (with minds that have already been burned by television, like a fuse) to imagine that their toy guns are real (as sophisticated as they have become, they remain toys), Fenix had the immense pleasure of entertaining himself with the concrete, authentic remnants of war: tanks, half-tracks, grenades, guns, loaded machine guns, bombs that hadn't exploded and which he and the other children, with perseverance, kept trying to disarm with scientific curiosity, or would open a big capsule from a cannon, hitting its ball against a rock to lay bare the compact gunpowder shaped like hollow macaroni. Since the matches were kept under lock and key due to scarcity, they would light them with magnifying glasses that would concentrate the sun's rays, to observe how the macaronis would devour themselves before being propelled through the shaft and disappearing into the air like fireworks. They played war, hurling grenades at each other; one of them ended up exploding in one of his friends' hands, and the neighbours finally noticed what the children were up to. The comments, like "He's lucky that it only took one hand" or "Yes, a little more and it would have killed him," were nothing more than variations of the phrase: "Lots of people don't even have this to eat."

However, as is often the case, the discipline ended up slackening. Moreover, on those warm summer nights, after dinner, with the windows open, who wasn't having an extra glass of wine, or a pitcher of beer? The world, as horrible as it had been over the last few years, with one or two extra shots, became more beautiful, and the "Peaceful Days" seemed to overtake their hearts. So, what could really happen to the children?

Fenix's father was probably always gone on business trips. Since the fistful of stones, his business had grown and he had now gotten involved in the contraband of cigarettes; but, before that, he needed to go through with the lighters, with their loads of fragrant smoke, and other smokers' accessories, including golden filters that weren't real gold. As a result, since there was no sun at night and the magnifying glasses were of no use, the responsibility fell on Fenix to provide the sacred fire for the macaroni gunpowder, which, they supposed, in the darkness, would produce even brighter fireworks. And one night, the little god that was Fenix's father, without ever finding out, lost one of the lighters that was carried in his son's pocket to a secret meeting in a secret location, a kind of ditch where they had hidden all the wastes of war that they considered useful for their entertainment and amusement.

That night, to go big, they prepared three shells whose macaronis would be ignited by the lighter instead of, tediously, one by one, with the magnifying glass. Thanks to the sacred fire, at night, the vulgar macaronis would shine in all their beauty with the luminous wake they would trace across the sky. And many from the city, anxious, expectant, came out for this special night: Fenix's cousins, and many other children from the neighbourhood, stood in front of the three long bulky capsules that contained the uncooked macaroni. How would they do it? One after the other? Or, would they light papers with the lighter, and one, two, three, set fire to the capsules? One, the wise member of the group, made an intelligent observation that suggested they proceed with caution: they had never simultaneously lit all the macaroni in one capsule, and didn't know what would happen. It would be better to light one of the macaroni first and see what would happen before continuing on with the others. They discussed: what could happen? Lighting one or a hundred would yield the same results, instead of one rocket, they would have a hundred, and it would be even more spectacular. To end the discussion once and for all, Fenix, owner of the sacred fire, tonight became a leader.

"Enough! I'm the one who brought the fire, so I'm the one who decides, and I've decided that we'll try it with just one first to see what happens."

And so he did. And he was lucky, he could tell whoever would listen, and he wasn't blinded or disfigured; a small tube of gunpowder wasn't the same as a whole pack of them, especially with them all compressed together in the capsule. He approached the flame of the lighter; maybe it was the strange hiss, the sound of the suction like a high-pitched whistle, which made him move his head away more quickly than the macaroni which, propelled by the unexpected explosion at the bottom of the capsule, shot out with a force and speed never before reached. And there was a unanimous "Ohhh" before the beauty of the flying tubes, which were more than flaming, red canes tracing a trail through the night. But the "Ohhh" quickly turned into a chorus of "Oh no!" and "What a disaster!" And yet, its beauty was mesmerizing; they hadn't planned for the tubes to reach two or three haystacks, or for the flames to run through the field toward the others, like suns illuminating the night, and they saw, up above, for the first time, he who was always motionless, dancing and jumping, spinning in circles, and, despite his reputation as a mute, also for the first time, they heard him sing (if those guttural sounds in which no words could be discerned could be called singing); the fool on the hill. The muffled cries of the city could be heard, along with the much louder church bells, but by the time the ancient fire truck had appeared, without water, ringing its bell with a festive energy so that people would let them through, the stacks had already burned to the ground. The only thing they managed to extinguish was the fool on the hill's dancing; they brought him to jail, convinced that he was the one who had set fire to the haystacks.

⟿ 15.

❦──**Fenix saw the** return of Judit's white bread; every
three or four days, she would knead in the kitchen and, the
next morning, very early, while everyone slept, would slice it
and bring it to the baker's, with a little "Jacobowicz" label on it.
It was usually Fenix who would go get it around midday, with
a white tablecloth. Big and round, it would rise so much that he
would carry it, wrapped in the tablecloth, hugging it close to
his chest like a loved one and, often, if it had risen quite a lot,
he would need to make another trip to go back and get the
mould. How and why it was kept fresh for two or three days,
this was another one of the secrets lost in the night of the times.

They returned to the habit of going to Sunday mass, taking a walk through the city square, and sitting at the tables of
the bakery despite the variety of the cakes being far from what
it was during the "Peaceful Days." The visits to the cemetery
stopped being regular. The houses needed to be rebuilt so they
could be liveable again (roofs caved in, doors dilapidated, windows stolen, and the lack of glass complicated things), a task
that forced the postponement of the restoration and maintenance
of the graves. "The dead aren't going anywhere," some said.

Judit had free time on Sunday afternoons. Without being able to speak of salary, when it occurred to the Mistress (employing, housing, and feeding her were already deeds that would earn her a place in heaven), she barely received any compensation for her work, with which she could do very little, unless she expected a large number of generous acts. And in the summer, Sunday was the day when they would go out to the field to play their games; to the forests to look for mushrooms in the shade and moisture of the trees; to pick flowers and, stomping on them, run, roll around on the ground and lay down in the grass.

One day, Judit, with a bulky bunch of red poppies, violets and other wildflowers in her hand, stood still and stiff like a statue and wouldn't respond to the impatient cries of "Let's go!" and pushes from Fenix. Judit stared at the bouquet, twirled it, and finally reacted:

"You know something, Fenix?"

"What?"

"I don't know when I'll have enough money to be able to buy a big bouquet of roses or carnations. Not even calla lilies or gladiolas."

"So?"

Judit looked at him, then at the flowers and, with a smile caught somewhere between sympathy and sadness, asked:

"Will you come with me to the cemetery?"

Fenix, frowning, his head tilted to one side, looked at her and pondered for a few seconds.

"Alright. Let's go."

To get there, they needed to cross town. But the city was small and Judit and Fenix's steps were quick.

The cemetery groundskeeper wasn't in his booth. Despite the requirements of social reorganization, maybe because it was Sunday, the dead could be content with so many visitors coming to decorate their graves, pull weeds, plant flowers or bring bouquets as their spiritual nourishment.

For Judit, whose trembling hand was holding Fenix's, it was hard to find the family grave, and if it weren't for the wooden cross with the inscription "Horvath family", she wouldn't have been sure that it was the right one, with the burial mound now sunk in and its level lower than the ground. The cracks were wide and deep; one could sink a leg into them, who knows to what depths. Judit, on her knees, hesitated in putting her bouquet down. She placed it on the side of the depression and her hands tried to level the earth and cover the cracks. She worked to the point of the impossible, to the point of desperation, to the point of rage until, wailing, she stopped and exclaimed: "It will never be a proper grave like the others! Never!" She bit her lip as though to hold back the waves of rage and envy that she knew to be sinful. Finally, still on her knees, she put down the flowers that she had brought and, joining her palms together, like a schoolgirl, prayed until she became calm.

With serene and silent tears, she stood up, took Fenix by the hand, and as they walked away, told him: "You know, Fenix, if it weren't for you, I'd want to be down there, with my family."

❧ 16.

❧——If social life was being reorganized, the institutions needed to be as well. No one had the slightest idea where the prosecutor who accused the fool on the hill of arson and pyromania, the jury, or the judge that would act as arbitrator had come from. The question was reasonable: in the small city, despite the existence of the gallows, there was no courthouse, and in this case the assembly room of City Hall would be used. Unfortunately, there were no first-hand witnesses of the event, and the children, some of whom were now much older, were not allowed inside, nor were they listened to. Believing that they wanted attention and to show off with an event that had never before been seen or that had never before occurred in the small city's history, no one paid any mind to the four or five children, including Fenix, who told the adults what had happened. Not even Judit believed him; with an "It probably only *seemed* like it was you," she put an end to the tale and sealed it with a kiss. Captain Vorosoff argued that it was an issue that pertained to civil justice as opposed to the military, since it wasn't caused by any event of war, not even sabotage.

From the comments he heard at home, his mother's, without
a clear accusation, was quite direct:

"Just hang him and be done with it."

His grandfather, who smoked many pipes, would drool
and every now and then say:

"No, I don't think it was him."

His father said nothing, or what he did say was consistent
with his lifestyle: he was always coming and going.

"Since I'm never here, I don't know what happened exactly.
I'm better off minding my business than giving an unjust opinion."

Try as he might, Fenix does not remember everything
exactly. Nor could he. For example, what was the opinion of
the general population, the infamous *vox populi*? The majority
didn't believe that it had been the fool on the hill. Those who
had known him for decades had never seen him do crazy things
of the sort, which is to say that he never did anything other
than stand motionless on the side of the hill for hours on end.
Moreover, where would he have gotten the matches, which
couldn't even be found in every home, to the point where many
needed to get embers ceded by one of their neighbours in order
to make a fire? This didn't mean anything; many had seen him
cooking on the riverbank or at the edge of the forest. Or
maybe, as mad as he was, he knew how to make fire by hitting
two rocks together, just like a caveman—which, after all, he
appeared to be.

There was another argument: that, if the haystacks were
poorly put together, after a rainfall or due to the humidity,
because of a lack of ventilation or an excess of fermentation,
they could have caught fire all by themselves. Unfortunately,
whoever was asked, "Have you ever witnessed that phenomenon?" with honesty, needed to answer no. Everyone knew that it
was possible, but no one could attest to it.

Regardless, the little city was abuzz. As though there hadn't been enough dead. Without counting those since the invasion of the Turks nor adding them to the last Germans that in the central square, thanks to the Russians, ascended to the heavens or descended into hell with their arms in the air, never had anyone seen the gallows taken out of storage, not even to dust it, and, therefore, the idea of seeing it in action filled the residents with excitement. It was an authentic antique; to be precise, it was mounted on four wheels, almost like mill wheels. From the platform arose the fateful *L*. Yes, a genuine authentic artisanal antique for which an American millionaire would pay a fortune, so long as it made history with a few hangings.

They took it out into the cobblestone courtyard that gave access to the old stables to see if it was in good condition and ensure that it hadn't been eaten by moths and termites. They found it looking decent enough, apart from the rope, which was dried out and no longer as sturdy. At least they realized it in time; what a spectacle it would have been for the executioner. What executioner? Officially, an employee of the police or the municipal justice system, with a fixed salary, there wasn't one. They called for a volunteer: twenty presented themselves. Since the courtyard gates were open during the day, the place became a tourist attraction for all ages, from children of 8 to 80, including Fenix's cousins and he himself, overcome with a morbid curiosity without a shadow of guilt, just like all human beings—a morbidity of which many, drugged, beg for more.

And so Judgment Day came. The biggest problem, people said, had been finding a gavel for the judge. Since they only remembered at the last minute, there was no time to make one, so they used a kitchen meat tenderizer, removing the metal part. The only person on the platform (behind a desk upon which,

on a little stick as a flagpole, they wanted to fly a little Czechoslovak flag, but couldn't get one), was the judge, wearing a
gown in which, with a little bad faith, one could notice holes
made by moths (unfortunately, in good faith as well). In front
of him, at the foot of the platform, to the right, behind a few
old tables with his folders and papers, in even older chairs, the
prosecutor and the defence attorney. The jury on the left, sitting in ordinary chairs. Among them, in the middle, like an
exhibition piece, guarded by two policemen, sitting on a stool
in handcuffs, the fool on the hill.

They say that the judge, before hitting the desk to impose
silence and open the session, frowning, sniffed the makeshift
gavel two or three times so loudly that it was enough to silence
the crowd that filled the assembly room and stifle the chuckles
of those who were aware of the origin of the instrument.

And the strike of the gavel resounded to open the court
session, which was relatively brief: the prosecutor accused the
fool, who, wearing dirty pants full of patches and a shirt in no
better condition, with his eyes dilated in fear and bewilder-
ment, stared at all the people surrounding him, still silhouettes
instead of trees or one of the landscapes he would look upon
from the top of the hill. His long, dirty beard reached his waist
and no one could make him remove his hat, made of an un-
recognizable material, under the ribbon of which he had pinned
a withered flower that he had pointed to a thousand times so
they could give him a fresh one. As the story goes, the jailer had
asked him what it was that he wanted and the fool, without
speaking, but occasionally mumbling something that sounded
like "Frol" or "Forl," continued pointing to it. The jailer wasn't
a bad man, he treated and fed him well, but he didn't give him
a fresh flower: he said he found the way he asked very funny,

especially how he pronounced the word. Hearing him speak was a privilege that no one had ever had.

The prosecutor accused the "person present" (since his name wasn't known; not even the fiercest threats from the police could get it out of him). The evidence was categorical and irrefutable: he was caught at the scene of the crime, *in flagrante*, which is to say "in the act," dancing madly and joyfully, and singing—in short, celebrating in a clearly sadistic way the damage that he had caused. His disdain toward those present, the judge, the jury, the public, humanity as a whole, proved it; his refusal to speak or take his hat off reinforced the aforesaid. As a result, he requested that his Honour and the members of the jury, so that these nefarious deeds, these targeted attacks on the goods of the community, wouldn't be repeated, apply all the weight of the law, *ergo*, that the accused—an extremely dangerous arsonist that had no respect ... etc., etc.—be put to death. And he would have continued speaking until today if the judge hadn't lowered his gavel with an energetic and resounding: "Thank you, Mr. Prosecutor."

The defence attorney argued that finding the "gentleman" at the scene of the crime was no proof that he was guilty, since the hill was his usual dwelling, which is to say, where he was most frequently seen; as for the dance, rather than "joy," in the words of the prosecutor, it was undoubtedly a reaction provoked by the phenomenon, and his alleged singing, cries of fear; that nothing was found on him that could have provoked the fire, that there are no witnesses. Furthermore, that there were whispers about the presence of children who seemed to know how the events unfolded, and that even though they weren't of legal age to make an official statement, interrogating them to clarify the unhappy situation was not against the law.

As a result, because of all the aforesaid and given that the accused (although there was no psychiatric evidence, which was a shortcoming of this process), it is perfectly well known and is *vox populi*, that he is not in his right mind, *ergo*, he was not responsible for his actions, and since there was no conclusive proof, he asked that they apply the benefit of the doubt to absolve the accused, *ergo*, give him his freedom.

The defence seemed solid. Agitation in the courtroom. The gallows, which everyone had pictured in the central square with someone hanging and swaying in the wind, seemed to fade from thought. The members of the jury were stunned. The judge needed to intervene.

"Gentlemen, please proceed with your deliberation and pronounce your verdict."

The jury disappeared behind a door. If before they retreated voices could be heard, sighs here and there, at this moment it seemed like the windows had been opened and a breeze of silence had invaded the assembly room.

When there are several stories surrounding a topic that appears to be simple—in this case, hanging an arsonist—people soon begin to grow tired. The jury took too long to return, and although their delay kept those present on edge for a time, after two or three comments which, although they had been made quietly, were heard by the entire room (even the judge frowned: "I don't know what the hell they're doing in there. What are they, members of parliament?" "Or politicians?" "Go on, say yes, guilty, and let's get on with it"), people started coughing in ways that sounded forced, stirring in their seats, tapping their feet on the floor until, *bam!*, a blow of the gavel and the judge's announcement put things in their place.

"Gentlemen, the jury."

They entered looking more preoccupied than they had when they had left. All of them, except one, the spokesman, took a seat. And the spokesman said:

"Your Honour, we have a problem that makes it difficult to decide with honesty and clear consciences." He became silent and bit his lips.

"Go on, what is the problem?"

"We don't know the law."

The defence attorney and prosecutor looked at each other, then looked at the judge who was scratching the back of his neck with the hand that was free of the hammer, which he sniffed again before asking:

"What law? Or rather, which of the laws? Neither I nor, I believe, these two gentlemen together, know the totality of the laws, which have never served much purpose, nor would we be able to guess which one you don't know and that you need to know to make a decision. Be more specific, please."

"One of us believes, and another has heard talk of, a law stating that if the guilty party doesn't confess to his crime, he cannot be condemned."

The first thing to break the silence and stillness that was produced in the room was the laughter with Homeric ambitions of the prosecutor, who stopped laughing only when it stopped coming out, in spite of his visible efforts to emit it.

"Ha ... ha .... ha .... It's the first time I hear something so stu ... excuse me, I mean, the mention of the possibility of the existence of a law of that nature. If it existed, humanity would be plagued with thieves, robbers, murderers, con men or worse, the entire world would be run by those kinds of people."

"And isn't it?"

Since the prosecutor had attracted the attention of the entire room, no one knew where the comment had come from. It is supposed that the judge had made it since many, for a few seconds, saw him cover his mouth with one hand.

The defence attorney limited himself to clearing his throat and:

"Your honour, I believe there is indeed a kind of law like that. Right now I can't recall exactly its number nor where ..."

"Ha ... a *kind* of law. Nice legal precision. And seriously! Your Honour, as a representative of the people here, who are hungry for justice, I beg of you to bring justice, for once."

"I agree," the defence attorney intervened. "I wouldn't dare to swear that this law exists, but I do know the law of the benefit of the doubt. It would be good and fair for us to give the accused the opportunity to speak. Please, put forth the question to the accused regarding his implication in the crime, and then we'll see."

Knowing him to be mute, those who defended the fool considered the attorney's suggestion (after the fact, clearly, when everyone becomes wise) to be a serious mistake.

The prosecutor shrugged and turned away from the fool. None of the members of the jury could speak to him. The lawyer approached him:

"Tell me, you poor soul, who people want to use for their amusement: were you the one who set fire to the haystacks? Simply tell me yes or no."

The fool looked at him as though he did not understand. The lawyer repeated the question. The entire room was in suspense. The fool stopped looking at the lawyer. The judge leaned over his desk and his whisper was heard by everyone.

"Yes, poor soul, such a poor soul, say no, say it isn't true, say no, no ..."

And the fool of the hill smiled, took his hat off and showed the judge the withered flower on the brim. The only thing that came out of his mouth was the word "Frol."

The judge remained in his seat, banged his gavel so violently that he made half the people in the room jump, dropped it to the side with rage and with his elbows on the desk, put his head in his hands.

Whether because of the comments he heard, or those that were distorted and became legends that he would hear when he returned to visit (forty years later maybe?), if Fenix needed to tell the story of this trial, he would need to piece it together like a puzzle, inexplicably.

The Russian army, headed by Captain Vorosoff, who was busy with other tasks, and the NKVD, which was busy with the cleansing of politicians (for example, finding some motive to incarcerate Fenix's father for the third time, since in a little police mind, there is only room for doubt and distrust), didn't stick their noses into the matter of the arson, which was a kind of parallel history lived by the city's residents, almost like a celebration, having forgotten that there even was a Russian army and an NKVD in action.

He tells the story that, with the violent blow of the judge's gavel, the matter was resolved, and even more so when, after rubbing his face and eyes, he stood up, took a tissue and, blowing his nose, disappeared into a back room.

The figures of the prosecutor and the defence attorney (they even knew his name) were familiar. But no one knew exactly where the judge had come from. They had probably brought him in from some major city since, just as he had never been seen before, he would never be seen again. This wasn't too serious of an issue: what was serious was that the final blow of his gavel, which would have relieved his soul, didn't conclude anything, didn't outline nor confirm any sentence and left several loose ends, a kind of emptiness. And, although the human mind almost always is, it cannot tolerate emptiness in its surroundings.

The story of the fool of the hill (after his performance before the judge, the idiot, to many people) rolled along as though on the wheels of the gallows. The prosecutor and defence lawyer collected their things, said goodbye effusively with a "Nice to see you, until next time," and left through the main door. The members of the jury were disappearing one by one, as though they were unhitching themselves. The fool of the hill was brought back to prison and, one day, it was announced that the new, freshly cleaned rope was ready for use.

By what decree or order, and from whom, did it come to this, no one knows. There were no official documents kept in any archives, no record; the entire trial had been oral and that is how, through word of mouth, the story was told. And until the eyes of the last witness shut forever, and his last breath carried what he remembered from the story, it would remain an urban legend.

There was no doubt about what happened next. If anyone (most of them) thought that the wheels would bring the gallows to the central square, they were wrong. Everything occurred in the stone courtyard where they had taken it and set it up; freshly painted and with a brand new rope, it was once more visited by all the residents of the city that could walk, including those who did it with crutches or canes.

And it happened one morning, at eleven o'clock. Children were not allowed to enter. At the gate, an employee of the only funeral parlour in town was collecting coins and bills in a top hat for the casket and the costs of the fool of the hill's burial. Afterward, people would say that there had been a mandatory entrance fee. When there was not even a square metre of free space left, the front gate was closed with difficulty and there was silence. The children that had climbed the fence and onto the roof of the stables, among them Fenix, had a privileged view of the show.

And the procession appeared: at the head of it the volunteer executioner, who would never be paid for this "official business." The fool of the hill followed him, accompanied by a priest, and behind them two police officers and, closing the parade, the jailer.

According to the priest, the fool refused to confess, so he could not absolve him of his sins. The most serious, the arson, didn't entitle him to a sacred burial. The children were indifferent to all this, but not to the events that followed; when he reached the gallows, the fool was asked for his last wish. Whether he understood the question or not, no one will ever know: what is certain is that he removed his hat and pointed to the dried flower. With tears in his eyes, the jailer climbed the two steps, carrying a beautiful red rose. He took the withered flower and placed the fresh one under the ribbon. A slight smile from the fool who, immediately, put his hat on. When they went to put the rope around his neck, with shrieks, he didn't allow them to take the hat off, gripping it with both hands, a whim of madness, according to many, that gave the executioner a futile task; forcing (no one wanted to help him), he first put one hand through, then the other, until the rope fit harmoniously around his neck like a collar that, despite the priest's firmness, wouldn't let him fall into hell. They invited him to climb a stepladder onto a tall stool. This made him happy, and once on top, he looked around with the widest possible smile; from this hill, he could see the field and trees.

The executioner shortened the rope until it was taut, tied it to a shackle and hesitated when the moment came to remove the stool with a kick until the audience, impatient ... The distance between the rope and the floor was too short (there was no other solution since the trap, because there was no well, couldn't be used) and the fool's body shook so violently that his hat fell off, until his open eyes continued staring forever at the field, the trees, the forest, the mythical fire that he didn't cause. His only tragic form of revenge: his tongue sticking out at everyone watching.

Given the priest's refusal, the nameless fool had a destiny other than being embraced by mother earth. The employees of the funeral parlour never told anyone how much money they had raised, and anyway, who would they tell? They put him in a common casket, without even closing his eyes, so that he wouldn't get lost on the way to Bratislava, the university they were bringing him to in a pickup truck. There they would receive him with all the honours of an unknown soldier for the march to progress and the future triumph of medical science: immortality.

The reorganization of life wasn't good news for everyone. The Hungarian language was banned everywhere. The school was being rebuilt, and at the beginning of September, Fenix would begin attending to study his first letters in a language that wasn't his mother tongue, but that wasn't foreign to him either: Slovak, which, due to the tension between the two sister tribes, they taught with a Czech accent. God only knows whether the difference really matters. This would be in September, and it was only the beginning of August; the peak of the summer. They had just finished sending the fool away and the peasants, in addition to preparing new haystacks for winter, were sharpening

their scythes to begin reaping wheat, the second harvest of another grain. Many were already searching for a pig for the Autumn slaughter and Fenix's grandfather would visit his vineyard
daily, and delicately feel the internal pressure of the grapes, in
order to pick them in their prime for winemaking.

If for the anxious, those who were avid for money, and the
grandfather (whose winery was now almost drained and the
barrels, when knocked on, sounded like shovelfuls of dirt hitting a coffin), a month was very little time, for the child that
Fenix was (or perhaps not so much a child anymore; he had now
seen many open eyes), this month seemed like an eternity.

— 17.

꧁——THE REORGANIZATION POSED other problems. Once the war was over, and the "Peaceful Days" had returned, it was impossible for the Mistress to find someone to, if not rebuild the house that was bombed, at least take care of the farm, sow, harvest and, with the priest's blessing, replenish the stable with a cow, and the coop with chickens, ducks and geese. The population had thinned, in the city just like the rest of the world, between those killed in the bombings, the Jews who were taken, those that, behind the illusions, had gone away to a better world, the husbands who escaped their wives (or, like her own husband who seemed to continue escaping, since he was never around), and those who went to the front, perhaps never to return. Labour, especially for field work, was lacking. And whoever could work, with all the work that there was to be done throughout the city, would never do so in the palace. It was *vox populi* that the Horvath family had lived like slaves, and that their deaths had freed them. The Mistress, frustrated and furious at not having found anyone, and maybe enraged with Horvath for having died without her permission, took revenge and punished Judit by kicking her out of the house and sending her to sleep in the basement, no matter what Fenix said or how much he kicked.

However, he didn't kick. There were no soldiers anymore, it was summer and the basement, that had once been hell, thanks to some disinfection, cleaning and tidying by Judit, became a perfect nest of paradise.

In a book of Chinese wisdom (it seems that most of the Chinese are wise) it is written that there are nine ways to make love, and the rest are nothing more than useless acrobatics to make it more difficult, if not ruin it. In Judit and Fenix's case, neither of the two had a book to help them ruin it: the discoveries were spontaneous and a consequence of the serene investigations of their bodies, sensual instruments sensitive to their hands. A way of relaxing that Fenix, like an indelible stamp, or a mandate engraved on his soul like in stone would bring him many problems in the future, in the search of a pillow beautiful enough to bring him closer to the only genuine lost Paradise. Can one speak of lovers' quarrels between a young woman like Judit, blessed with peasant strength, and a child like Fenix, from a comfortable family? For some reason, especially during the summer nights when the lover descends secretly as though it were something forbidden (his mother didn't even notice), after the fights softened by pillows, there was no greater delight in the world than resting between Judit's thighs, hugging one of them, his head on the patch of clovers more delicious than a feather pillow, napping and, every now and then, feeling the other thigh wrap around him, or brush against him, provoking sparks of pleasure on his skin.

Sundays, little by little, became days of celebration again. Although not sufficiently, according to the priest, the number of parishioners was increasing. One of the towers that had fallen during the passage of the front still hadn't been fixed, and many feared the collapse of the other. The dead in the cemetery were visited more often. And just as the graves were refurbished, headstones and slabs of stone were ordered that, along with the other repairs, generated more local business. The bakery's selection increased a little but it wasn't complete enough to justify sitting there, except for an ice cream that was a little watery, but helped beat the heat. Whether Fenix's father was home or not, the lunches returned and the grandfather, as though nothing had happened in the last while, after two or three glasses of wine, with his pipe smoking, would sit in the living room in his usual armchair.

Fenix wouldn't stay in the living room anymore to watch his grandfather fall asleep smoking his pipe or humming a tune, like his favourite song: "*Oh, death*, ..." No, several August days had gone by, and summer found itself threatened not only by a few yellow leaves that had already appeared as the first signs of autumn, but ruined by school: the start of classes was approaching. He didn't go play with his cousins or friends either; for that, he had all the days of the week.

Yes, Sundays, maybe the last warm Sundays, needed to be taken advantage of. Especially with Judit having those free afternoons. They were days of freedom. And even if, in the peak of winter, they could also have them when they went sledding or skating on the lake, it wouldn't be the same. With the amount of people that would go, solitude and intimacy would be impossible. And even so, how would they be able to enjoy it in the cold weather?

However, summer was a sacred season; it had made possible Fenix's discovery of the clover patch, which, like a dark cloud on two pillars, surrounded by a skirt, a widely accessible cave, would jump on top of him and, maybe due to its colour,

stood out among the other white or grey hued clouds that drift-
ed across the celestial dome.

It was probably one of those Sundays, if not the very last
one of the month. There were no more wildflowers, and Judit
never again expressed her desire to go back to the cemetery.
When Fenix asked about it, she told him that she was saving
money for the Day of the Dead, when she hoped to buy flowers
and candles. They knew that it was useless to search for raspberries or blackberries, but maybe they would find mushrooms
if there was a lot of humidity or if it had rained that week. And
with absolute certainty, in the light of the sun that illuminated
everything, better than the one in the basement, they would go
find four-leafed clovers in faraway places, even if they didn't
know them.

Among the things that returned, thanks to his father's new
trade as professional contrabandist, the chocolate that had
once, in time immemorial, brought Judit back to life, reappeared. And his mother, as though she were a priest and the
chocolate, a piece of the body of Christ, after every dinner or
lunch, broken off from a bar, would place in Fenix's mouth a
piece almost as thin as a host and that would melt at the same
speed, fading, and leave him frustrated in his desire to receive
more, as well as his inability to bring his lover his dark and
sweetened tongue. Ah, but Fenix had grown; the war, the
adults, had taught him, even without meaning to. After a
minutious search (his mother was very skilled at hiding things),
he would find her hiding place and—he wasn't stupid, he acted
with prudence—stole two pieces, a small one for the week and
a bigger one to set aside for Sunday.

And another Sunday arrived, one that they hadn't been
expecting.

So much has been said and written about the spontaneity and joy of living that it has ended up killing them or, at least, made us doubt that they really exist. Since, in Fenix and Judit's case, it would be an exaggeration to speak of the Golden Age, but rather only of the resurrection of the "The Joyous Peaceful Days of Old" during which they both, without thinking that it was in a spontaneous way, ran through the meadow, frolicked in the grass, where she would deny Fenix the patch in which he searched for the lucky clover, and where he, in turn, denied her the piece of chocolate, where she needed to chase him and catch him to receive it in exchange for the clover, or fall in his arms, roll around and search for it, often in Fenix's mouth.

There was a time when, over the course of these adventures, to catch Judit and pull her onto the ground, Fenix needed to expend the energy of a titan. But he had now grown and Judit couldn't get away from him very easily. And it was as though the world had been turned upside down. Limited by her long skirt, surpassed by Fenix's strides and jumps, in the interest of obtaining the chocolate, it was she who needed to make the greater effort.

To shorten the distance between them so that Judit could reach him when her desire for chocolate came to a head (who knows if it was really for chocolate or, increasingly intense with the years, for some subtle perfume like the one that made Fenix's grandfather gallop through mountains and valleys), Fenix needed to slow down.

That day, Judit was chasing him at the edge of the forest on a path bordered by a pasture that was used for who knows what; the trees whizzed by. And when the desires peaked, just when he was about to slow his pace, a fragment of silence went through him like a lightning bolt, the wave of the explosion propelled him forward, making him lose his balance and roll onto the ground.

Dizzy, he didn't react right away. First on his knees: nothing. Staggering, he stood up; with his heart beating fast, he searched for her: Judit had disappeared from the horizon. All he could see was a well, and yellow leaves swaying as they fell.

⚘ 18.

⚘——Fenix didn't require an explanation: he had lived through a war, and played at it enough as well. Not even the fool of the hill's sentence had held him back. And, as though this would have encouraged he and the other children, taught them some kind of lesson, in spite of the explanations of how an anti-personnel or anti-tank mine worked, and of the warnings of what they needed to do if they found one—notify the police, what few policemen they could find— they preferred to make them explode by hurling rocks at them from a hill. It was entertaining and they knew perfectly well what the consequences of an explosion were. And so he knew immediately what the consequences of the sound he heard would be. A story tragically repeating itself. The adults didn't believe that there were still anti-tank or anti-personnel mines buried in the field. It was as though, now that the war was over, they would have miraculously disappeared, as though their warnings were enough to make them. There weren't even that many buried to worry about. What kind of German had the foolish idea of putting mines in the middle of the field or along the side of the path? What happened was pure bad luck, negligence most likely due to ignorance.

Fenix had no doubt about what had happened. He didn't run over, not because of the danger of stepping on another one, but because he dreaded finding what he already knew was there, or because of his hope of hearing a voice (a wail, or several, slow, full of shock at what had happened). He approached slowly. He reached the pit that the explosion had made and turned toward the meadow. He climbed in slowly, very slowly, and when he saw her—how can he explain this, how can he talk about what he felt, describe Judit in her absolute stillness and silence? It is enough to say that those open eyes, golden like the autumn leaves, took in the sun without blinking: Fenix, having seen it other times, too many for a child, knew exactly what it meant.

And he ran, he ran blind, he screamed, he cried out, he doesn't even remember to whom. Maybe terror is what propelled him, maybe the possibility of help, or the resurrection before the final judgment came.

He entered into his house with a howl that made the walls shake, and if it didn't wake the dead from their graves, it certainly woke up the grandfather and caught the attention of his mother, who, on the same veranda, grabbing him by the shoulders, began to shake him: "What happened? What sort of mischief did you get up to?" Almost out of breath, as though his soul were escaping every time he desperately cried out her name, he couldn't speak, he couldn't explain. His mother shook him violently, grabbing him by the shirt, and the slaps soon followed; limp and empty like a puppet, Fenix couldn't defend himself from them. His father was absent; the beating his son was receiving (because he loved someone, and was loved in return?) were probably actually meant for him. Now, Fenix couldn't even finish screaming the word that was being interrupted with a blow every time he tried to shout it: "Jud ...! Jud ...!"

His grandfather tried to intervene. He was thrown out with an insult that must have been referring to some past sin or crime, since he didn't insist and, like a frightened dog, disappeared with his tail between his legs. But the person who everyone had forgotten, who would have been reading or napping at the time, was Captain Vorosoff, who, without being able to run because of his increasingly bulky belly, finally reached Fenix and his mother, who seemed to want to beat his soul out of him. And, while with his left hand he politely covered his mouth while yawning, with his right he pushed the barrel of the Luger into the Mistress's temple. At first, blinded, she seemed to think it was a fly, but after shaking her head and realizing that it wasn't going away, she stopped cold and looked out of the corner of her eye.

Who knows whether Captain Vorosoff really would have shot her; she didn't want to find out. She pushed Fenix away and left the room.

A few seconds of hesitation. The Captain put away the Luger, crouched down slightly and extended his arms. Fenix approached; sheltered, protected, consoled, he folded himself over his belly, and what had up to this moment been impossible occurred: he began to cry. Vorosoff brought him to his bedroom. There he set him down in an armchair and did what he considered appropriate for any man in his state: he served him a glass of vodka, which burned his throat. Fenix coughed; his mouth, pharynx and oesophagus were smouldering, and in his stomach a lake of fire formed that he was able to extinguish thanks to a glass of water that the Captain gave him as he sat down in front of him.

Fenix calmed himself. He stopped crying. With the tears still in his eyes and the same tightness in his throat, even though he spoke Slovak fluently, he slurred his speech, and his words were unclear (Vorosoff had many questions), as he told him what had happened. On a few occasions, with some urgency, he had seen the Captain appear by his bedroom door, go through the veranda, and bolt down the stairs. But this time, the Captain had to make an effort to get up since, two or three times as he tried to stand, it seemed that his belly was making him sit back down. In the end, biting his lip, as though he were trying to lift a large rock, he stood up. The man knew perfectly well that it was useless to rush, that arriving ten minutes, half an hour, or an hour later, was all the same. They weren't in the steppes of Russia and here, in the forests, and in the fields especially, there were no wolves or wild dogs. Vorosoff gently shook his head, then stopped and sighed deeply.

If he had needed to prepare an official ceremony, his movements would have been lighter and more precise. Now, more than because of his belly, they seemed slowed by the weight of life, which always entails death. Solemnly, he searched for his hat with the red star on it, which he put on in front of the mirror of his vanity without looking at himself much, not even to smooth his moustache, which was subtly similar to the Great Comrade's. He adjusted his stomach and belt. This time, perhaps more than usual, for courage, he served himself a glass of vodka, looking distracted, and performed the routine gesture of raising it up to Stalin's face, then downed it in one sip, approached Fenix, rubbed his hair and said "Come," made him stand up and directed him with one of his clumsy paws on his shoulder.

While they descended the stairs he gave a loud order, and the sub-officer with a few soldiers ran over to the half-track, which looked increasingly rickety. Once in motion, and in front of the stairs, Vorosoff picked Fenix up and sat him next to the driver, while he sat down behind him. He started the vehicle and the tank, which would follow the half-track like an older brother, followed this time as well.

Fenix directed them. All the commander needed was for him to point toward where Judit's broken body lay, and he didn't allow him to come with him into the meadow. He went out and came back without his hat, wiping his forehead with a dirty handkerchief, and looked at Fenix who, with his pupils dilated, was waiting for a miraculous announcement that would refute what he knew to be true, that would bring her back. No, instead of an announcement, he received two palms on his cheeks and a kiss on his forehead. Vorosoff's moist eyes stared into Fenix's; they remained this way for a while, until suddenly, as though the Captain had just remembered why he was there, he went back over to the sub-officer and spoke to him quietly. The officer headed toward the half-track, gave another order to one of the soldiers and with his help, pulled out a sheet and brought it into the meadow. The commander let them finish the task and climbed into the tank with Fenix, made the driver get out so he could take control, and then drove them back to the palace where they locked themselves in Vorosoff's room. Vorosoff then, as though to celebrate something, or drown his bitterness (the remedy is the same), made two glasses of vodka disappear. He offered one to Fenix, who had sat down in the same place as before, but with a "Thank you very much," he declined.

The drinks didn't appear to soothe the Captain; taking strides of almost seven leagues, he was pacing back and forth through the bedroom under Fenix's bitter gaze. He would stop every now and then to console him with affectionate little taps on his shoulders and caresses on his head. Although he remained the military commander of the little city, because of the NKVD, the civilian, municipal and police forces that had been restructured—which didn't matter much to him since, with the war over, his departure and return home were near—and although death was a daily occurrence, and Judit's, if it weren't for the existence of this child he had in front of him, was just one more, one of many, the uncertainty of whether Judit's accident was a civilian or military matter unsettled him.

There was a knock on the door: it was the sub-officer announcing the arrival of the half-track, asking for orders on the next steps to take with the remains of the "young lady."

"Wait!" and he slammed the door shut.

More pacing back and forth, until, having reached a decision, he stopped in front of Fenix.

"Do me a favour, go get your mother."

Fenix stood up. He stared at the Captain as though to ask him what on earth he was going to do with his mother, turned his head in order not to lose sight of the captain as he went toward the door, and just as he was about to turn the handle, Vorosoff sighed and said:

"You're right, since your mother is a witc … I mean, since she's very hot-headed, maybe you'd better go get your grandfather instead."

"If he's still here."

He found him in the living room in his favourite armchair, but he wasn't sleeping. More than smoking, he was nervously chewing on his pipe. He suspected that something out of the ordinary had transpired and had stayed. Without a word, apart from letting out a puff of smoke as though it would help him hear better, his eyes two question marks, he leaned forward when he saw Fenix appear, saying:

"Grandfather, the Captain wants to speak to you."

His grandfather jumped onto his feet:

"To me? What does he want? I didn't do anything."

"I don't know, grandfather. I'm only telling you what he told me."

The grandfather walked with a firm step but, due to guilt from the past or illegal errors of the present, he jogged behind Fenix as though he had aged 20 years all at once, to the point that touching him with a finger would be punishing him with absolute injustice.

Once in Vorosoff's bedroom, although he would have preferred a glass of *pálinka*, he accepted the vodka he was offered. The captain asked him if he knew what had happened, and told him. The grandfather listened, swallowing saliva and glancing every now and then at sorrowful little Fenix. Once he finished telling the story, the captain lowered his head.

A prolonged silence. Although reassured for his own safety, recuperating the 20 years he had aged on the walk over, Fenix's grandfather said, impatiently:

"So …?"

Vorosoff looked up at him.

"Did Judit have relatives? Do you know them? Where are they?"

"No, in this city, she had no one left."

He told him about the deaths of Judit's parents and brothers.

"In terms of others from the town they originally came from, I have no idea. From what I've heard, they were from the country, inland, from a place where there were too many Slovaks persecuting them, and they sought refuge in this city where the majority of the population is Hungarian. I don't know if he was a landowner or a simple wage-earning peasant, but …"

The captain raised his hand to indicate that he had said more than enough.

"Where is Judit's family buried?"

"In the city's cemetery."

And finally:

"Do you know where?"

"If the wind hasn't taken the cross, or it hasn't rotted, it would be easy to find the grave. Maybe, despite all the confusion there's been over the past while, they're even registered in the cemetery records."

"Very well. I'll make all the arrangements. Locate the grave by tomorrow afternoon. Ah, and although it never seemed to me that Judit was very educated or knew that God doesn't exist, I suppose she practised some kind of faith. Look for a priest from whatever religion that is. Since you're all capitalists, I'll pay for the sorcerer's hocus-pocus."

Fenix's grandfather said goodbye and left through the door, followed by Vorosoff who, implicating the mother of his assistant with the folder, cursed his absence due to his day off. He had a few words on the discipline of those drunks who were lazing around, and left through the veranda door to speak, in a whisper, with the sub-officer. The officer nodded a few times, raised his hand to his head in a salute, and then disappeared.

Once he was back, he called Fenix over and told him:

"I suppose that your father still hasn't returned, since he would already have called me to have a few drinks and play chess if he were here. You're a young man now, so I expect of you everything I would expect of a man. Today I have company, so I can't take care of you. Go wherever you want to distract yourself or to think about Judit, who, I guarantee you, we will take good care of and put in a good place so that she may rest in the way she deserves. But you can cry if you want as well; that is also something that men do. Tomorrow morning, if your father isn't back, I'll take you with me into the city, alright?"

"Alright, Captain," he said, and he raised his hand up to his imaginary cap.

Vorosoff smiled back at him. He stood up, accompanied Fenix to the door and before saying goodbye, told him:

"If you don't want to tell your mother anything, don't. And if she touches even a hair on your little head, let me know. Is that clear?"

"Very clear, my captain."

"Now go on, little rascal, and you can stop with all the Captain business."

His mother didn't ask him anything. She had already heard everything from her father, who, once he returned home, told the story in two taverns, which was the equivalent of telling the entire city and, at church, told the priest, to whom he paid a visit. And the city residents, as interested as they were in gossip, didn't worry much about the kind of news that, although not ordinary, was not exceptional either. There was no shortage of comments: "Fenix was lucky to avoid the mine. He could have died too." "Poor girl, she's better off dead, spending the rest of her life without legs would be awful."

—❦ 19.

❦——**THE FOLLOWING MORNING**, since his father hadn't appeared, without even asking his mother's permission, apart from sending her son to let her know, the Captain brought Fenix to the general command quarters located at City Hall. In a smaller office next to his own, he sat him down in front of a desk facing a chessboard that was already set up and gave him a book filled with chess problems to resolve in two or three moves. Fenix, from having watched the games that his father played against Vorosoff so many times, already knew how to play a little, but even if he could recognize some letters, he was far from knowing how to read and even less so the Russian Cyrillic characters.

Regardless, he didn't get intolerably bored; while the captain kept busy in his office, he played a few games, looked over papers, flipped through a few magazines that he found on the table and in the desk drawers, got up a few times to look out the window at the city square, and thus he managed to smother the waves of sadness that would come over him seemingly out of nowhere, and succeeded in holding back his tears. However, there was something more, something that he had never felt before in his life. Judit had been with him since he had first opened his eyes and, although he wasn't constantly "stuck to her skirt," so to speak, he could always count on her presence. And if at any time, for some unknown reason, he received a breath from the great beyond, like the ones that everyone receives but that not everyone perceives, a shudder, maybe of fear, he had always been able to count on a shelter to take cover in or a warm thigh to cling to; now, in addition to the waves of sadness, he felt, without seeing it, a strange veil covering him, in which he found nothing, absolutely nothing to hold onto. For the first time in his life, without being fully conscious of it, he experienced the solitude that, with highs and lows, would accompany him for the rest of his life.

Around noon, the assistant with the folder entered, this time indeed holding a folder, and a fairly bulky one at that. Captain Vorosoff, the general commander, requested little Fenix's presence.

Fenix followed him. Next to the captain's desk, a round table: two plates, a pair of fried eggs in each, two bread rolls, a bottle of vodka, two empty glasses, two glasses of water and, in one of the two chairs, Vorosoff, who was waiting for Fenix to join him for lunch.

The captain served him half a glass of vodka. Fenix, who vaguely remembered the glass from the day before, the infernal burn and the nausea it caused, nausea that he confused with the nausea of desperation (and a relief, as well, something that could help him tolerate the pain?), he could say that this second glass, now taken out of his own free will, was the first blurry letter of his school of alcoholism, which would gain a more precise outline in the last years of his life, when solitude would take shape once again. Already a model student, he toasted with his teacher and, emulating him, downed the vodka in one shot, which he quickly chased with the water. While the folder assistant came and went, they ate in silence, occasionally looking up at each other to smile, as much as their respective states of mind permitted. When they finished eating, still in silence, Fenix pointed to the bottle, and in silence, the captain shook his head no, then took it, raised it, and greeted Fenix's grandfather who was standing behind Fenix with Vorosoff's assistant.

"So?" Vorosoff asked.

"I spoke with the cemetery groundskeeper," the grandfather said. "The grave has been located and it won't be a problem to use it again for Judit. Enough time has gone by."

"And the sorcerer?"

"The priest? There's no inconvenience as long as we let him know in advance."

"How much notice does he need?"

"He said that these days, he's flexible."

Vorosoff turned to his assistant.

"Everything ready?"

"Everything ready, Captain."

"Good, we'll leave here at two thirty to go to the cemetery," he said, then he turned to the grandfather: "Please, let the priest know. Three o'clock at the cemetery. Before you go, a drink?"

The grandfather didn't resist.

Fenix waited in front of the chessboard with his forearms on the table and his head resting on them. At two thirty, the assistant needed to wake him up. Staggering a little, with Fenix in front and the assistant behind, they left the little office to fetch Vorosoff in the other. The captain led the way from his office to the stairs, then out the front door, where they found the half-track waiting for them with the coffin.

They climbed in. The half-track pulled out, turned at the city square and made its way to the cemetery. Fenix felt as though he were dreaming. He stared at the coffin made of unvarnished wood; he imagined Judit inside and asked himself: Were her eyes open? Would they be able to look at each other one last time? He didn't dare speak; he only listened to the sound of the half-track's engine, and the tracks of the tank behind them.

And another sound, of which it might be better not to speak, but it could indeed be heard: the road was bumpy and although the half-track's rocking from side to side didn't move the coffin itself because of the stops they had put to hold it in place, the coffin's interior still made muffled sounds at each jerk, knocking sounds that made Fenix think Judit was suffering and that any minute she would cry out: "Enough! Get me out of here! I can't take it anymore!"

The grandfather, the priest and the gravedigger with a shovel were all waiting in the booth of the front office. The half-track stopped and the driver waited for instructions. Since they couldn't all climb in, only the grandfather did to show them where to go. The graves prevented the advance of the half-track. The coffin didn't have handles. The driver and sub-officer carried it on their shoulders. The grandfather followed closely behind with two shovels.

By the time the priest had arrived with the gravedigger, the sub-officer, and the driver, they had already dug a hole in the soft earth in which to put the coffin, and were awaiting orders; the knocking together of bones interrupted them. The captain watched, with his hand on the barrel of his gun, biting his bottom lip: no, not all the dead had the same value. A shudder in his entire body and he ordered them to lower the coffin. The priest, with a book in his hand and an aspergillum in the other, flung a few drops of water, while mumbling who knows what; it was fairly brief.

And so the shovelling began. A corpse is a corpse, but a corpse underground is its definitive disappearance. Yes, we know it's there, but that distance, that layer of earth, seems infinite. Fenix was crying. The captain grabbed him by the shoulder and pulled him in close. There, together with her parents and brothers, Judit would rest until the day of the final resurrection. Everyone made the sign of the cross—even the captain, who, like any good educated communist, didn't believe in any of that nonsense.

They put the same old cross back in its place and under a clear sky, under the setting sun, with the dry leaves crunching under their shoes, they returned on foot to the gate and the office booth where the half-track was waiting for them.

—❧ 20.

❧——**PERHAPS BECAUSE OF** his father's frequent absences, to free him from the clutches of his mother's talons, the commander adopted Fenix like a son. Without a regular schedule, but practically every day, he would send for him and bring him with him to the command headquarters. The captain usually travelled in the half-track, although Fenix preferred the tank with the commander at the wheel. Vorosoff would happily oblige. Because of the noise that it made, the rust that was eating away at it, even the air that entered through holes and cracks, it looked more like a model from the First World War. But Fenix's imagination compensated for all the deficiencies and pretended to fire the cannon and machine guns in the back, though their hole had been plugged.

At the command headquarters, as soon as they arrived, before putting him in the office with the chessboard, Vorosoff would bring him to a locked room located at the back of the hall. He would open it with his key, and once inside, from a huge basket full of hay that he would rummage through, he would take two eggs, one for him and one for Fenix. Then the captain would close the door, they would return to the command headquarters office and from there, perforating the ends with a pencil and sucking through one of the holes, they would eat the raw eggs that made Fenix's stomach turn, though he would not complain. The captain would assure him that there was no food healthier or more nutritious in the world. If he knew anything about the high protein content of eggs, according to modern science, he knew nothing of the toxic elements in the whites if they aren't cooked, and the extremely high level of cholesterol in the yolk, inducer of heart attacks. In any case, although Vorosoff had eaten raw eggs since he was a small child, and would continue doing so, he would not die of a heart attack.

While he kept busy with his duties and obligations, he would always put Fenix in the side office, which turned out to belong to the assistant with the folder, who would appear every now and then, look over a file, remove some papers and put some more in, and then disappear again. In addition to the chess board, probably taken from the bookshop in the city square that never reopened its doors, he would provide him with colour pencils, notebooks to draw in, a pencil sharpener, and a box with a sliding lid to keep them in that he would later use in school. Perhaps because it formed part of his uniform just like his shiny medals, or because it symbolized his authority and dignity, or because of the pride of having taken this precious item from a German officer, in the command headquarters, he refused to let him touch the Luger.

Although there were several days left before the fixed date that human beings had decided was the official beginning of autumn, which does not mean much for the history of the Earth, which has it begin whenever it feels like it, with the reorganization of life nearly complete, the first day of September seemed to mean everything to the residents of Ipolyság, including the beginning of classes for Fenix. And since the commander's schedule wasn't marked by his duty so much as the amount of vodka consumed at the bar the night before, either alone or in the company of other officers who would join him, in order to be punctual and arrive at school on time, Fenix needed to return to his condition as a civilian.

Very early in the morning, accompanied by his cousins if they happened to leave at the same time, though it had never occurred to them to agree on one (curiously, Fenix preferred to go alone, since that way, he could feel the pain and presence of Judit more profoundly), with the days becoming increasingly shorter and colder, he would cross the two bridges that were still made of wood, climb the slope that brought them to the first level of the city, where the school could be found, next to a church.

Nevertheless, regularly, given that he went to school in half-day shifts, morning and afternoon, he often didn't go back home for lunch and would go visit Vorosoff, to be lifted in the air, folded over his belly, hugged, and kissed, and he would eat with him, the only person who would ask him how school was going. And it was going very well: since modern pedagogical education theories and their beneficial influence had not yet reached this remote world, located far away from large metropolitan cities, one month after beginning classes, he could already spell somewhat, and could already decipher any word (although he couldn't always understand their meaning). With a bit of an effort, he could already scribble full sentences like "Mother kneads the dough in the kitchen," a mystery beyond just the words since, apart from giving instructions to Judit, he had never once in his life seen his mother knead. After Judit's disappearance, a prematurely aged woman replaced her—or maybe she really was old, who knows, whom Fenix, who usually ate in the kitchen, would avoid like the plague because of her slobbery kisses and her rancid odour, far from the freshness of Judit's moist grass. To avoid her, he acted like a little prince: he would make her serve him in the dining room, even at breakfast.

Only years later would Fenix realize that Czechoslovakia wasn't completely communist yet, which explained why at school they had a weekly hour of religious studies taught by a nun. With these classes, his vague ideas about immortality, heaven, and hell, and who would go where and why, became clearer. He had an unpleasant surprise when the nun made them draw the lips of the seven deadly sins; comparing the drawings with his lips in the mirror, lips that were very nicely shaped and, to the best of his memory, very similar to Judit's, he realized that they both belonged to the order of sinners, and that they would go to hell for their lust.

At one of their lunches, he told the captain about his fear and worry. The captain became outraged for an infinite number of reasons, including the shame of religious teachings in schools, Catholic in this case, when there were so many other religions among the children in the city, like Russian Orthodox, not to mention the Protestants. But that it was even more shameful that they would teach these stupidities and lies that had already been debunked by science.

"So, Captain, there's no heaven?"

"No heaven, no hell. Fabrications from the priests to exploit and rob the people along with the capitalists. As Comrade Lenin said: Religion is the opiate of the masses."

Fenix remained quiet, but strangely so; so quiet that the captain, with his mouth now shut, felt the silence intensify, until only the sound of tears rolling over Fenix's cheeks could be heard. The captain, as though he were in a mass at the moment when the priest raises the host up to the Lord, didn't speak, and only limited himself to silently inquiring with an almost imperceptible movement of his head, and two question marks in his eyes.

"It's just ... it's just that, Captain, that means ... that means that I'll never see Judit again, not in heaven, or in hell."

At another lunch, he informed him that, according to his teacher, an order had arrived, he wasn't sure where from, for a collection of iron, that everyone needed to participate in. He wasn't a relative nor some generous uncle, but this is how Vorosoff treated him:

"It's definitely an order from Comrade Stalin. It's because Russia is lacking iron." He leaned over to say confidentially: "Comrade Stalin will appreciate and be grateful for your participation."

Fenix made a comment that disconcerted the Captain:

"It's a shame that you didn't arrive before the Germans who took all the iron from my father's workshop."

With the participation of the teachers, all the students, many volunteers, police officers, and the Red Army trucks, the task was completed in one day, on a Saturday. In organized groups, street by street, they practically "painted" the little city. The group that Fenix was part of knocked on the doors of every house. And as though it were a campaign for poor children in Africa, they would ask for something, a donation of some kind, to rebuild the industry that was lacking raw material, and in this way, make life even better than it was in the "The Joyous Peaceful Days of Old." Since everything would go into the same crucible, everything that was metal was accepted without discussion; from broken spoons, forks, and knives, to lucky horseshoes hung over the doors of houses. Those who had taken theirs down in time didn't have enough to erase the trace it had left behind. The rest was the job of the officers. Nothing was saved, not even what wasn't in sight. It is said that the biggest and most disgraceful scandal was with the city's two blacksmiths, who almost had to start another war to save their anvils.

The loaded trucks brought all the metal to the station, where the wagons on the platform were already waiting for the tanks, the remains of planes, cannons, and everything that was left over from the war that had entertained the children so much.

During lunch one day, when Fenix told the captain about the mission accomplished, he asked him another question that also complicated Vorosoff's life, but this time from a moral point of view, if not technical or philosophical.

"Tell me, Captain, the caps of beer bottles, aren't they made of iron? I'm asking because there was a discussion on the subject among those who were leading us; some said that they didn't see a reason why not if it was metallic matter, and the others said that yes, but a material so fragile that burned and evaporated in the blast furnaces, although they were metal, would only hinder the melting process."

"How do you know all this?"

"All this, what?"

"About the blast furnaces and the melting process."

"The teacher explained it to us, with pictures and everything."

"Aha, well then. And the teacher didn't say anything about the beer caps?"

"No, nothing. What do you think?"

Vorosoff scratched the back of his neck.

"I don't know, I have no idea. But I'll look into it and let you know."

⟿ 21.

Whether he looked into it or not, Fenix would never know; what is certain is that he never told him. Moreover, that lunchtime meeting, rather than the "Last Supper," could have been titled the "Last Lunch": he would never see Captain Vorosoff again; he would die that same night.

That evening, after having lunch with Fenix, Captain Vorosoff received two pieces of news. The first: with the war over and cleansing operation complete, he and his army were to return to Russia. They would leave in two days. The second: he could return home with a higher rank, as a Hero of the Soviet Union and the Red Army.

In spite of his volume, the Captain was bursting with joy. That night, he invited his comrades, the officers from his division, to the bar, to celebrate both events. As the story goes, in addition to eating like a bear, he drank like a sponge; even worse, he didn't limit himself to vodka, the pure spirit, but a variety of *pálinkas*, wines, and liquors that no doubt created a bad mix that was the principal cause of the accident.

No, there was no way he would accept that they drive him; drunk as a skunk, but convinced that he was completely sober, to return home, he insisted on driving by himself the tank that usually escorted him and that had now become a kind of lap dog.

The bridge's sturdiness had been guaranteed, tested by the Stalin T34 tanks, but no one had tried to ram into the guard-rails. Why the one Vorosoff was driving diverted so abruptly, if he had had a heart attack or if he was frightened by a hallu-cination of a tank coming from up ahead or a Stuka that was going to drop a bomb on him, no one will ever know, but what is certain is that he rammed straight through the rail into the river which, at this spot, limited and accelerated by the arches of the bridge that enclosed it, was deeper than anywhere else. All that could be seen of the tank was the back machine gun that was sticking out like the tail of a dog.

That night, it was an armoured casket for Vorosoff. In the morning, when Fenix went by and saw the broken guardrail, a police officer directing pedestrians, the commotion in the river, rubber dinghies, planks of wood, a tank, a crane over the shore, officers, and soldiers, he asked the policeman what had hap-pened. "Nothing, this is none of your business. Move along," and turned away from him to take care of the other curious onlookers, in increasing numbers, that had come to see some-thing that looked like a variation of the war.

Fenix considered himself mature enough to, if they didn't stop him by force or didn't notice him, choose his own path. Moreover, a sense of foreboding, a feeling of absence, an empti-ness in his house, the absence of the tank, of the half-track, of Vorosoff himself who, lately, had been sleeping late, took hold in him; with a knot in his stomach, he slid down the slope near the bridge and landed by the river. The officers on the river-bank, the expectant faces, watched the labour of the soldiers, one in a rubber dinghy and the other on the logs and planks of wood that they had put down leading up to the tank. With iron levers, they forced the hatch until, with a *crack*, as though they were opening the gates of hell, it opened. From the reaction of the soldiers who looked inside, only to turn away immediately, it was clear that not even a bubble would have made it out of the flooded interior.

Suddenly, all that could be heard was the flow of the river: the soldiers had removed their hats and the officers their caps. Was this the infamous moment of silence? Fenix wasn't sure, but he supposed so. And as he, too, removed his hat, he experienced the first terrible chill he had ever felt.

Fenix didn't count how long the silence lasted. The caps and hats resumed their position and an order could be heard. Despite the distance, when they pulled Vorosoff's body from the tank, Fenix could see his mouth hanging open excessively wide; he had probably, while the tank flooded, attempted to take a bite of air, and instead he bit into eternity.

Fenix didn't stay. He wasn't interested in seeing the last look in Vorosoff's eyes; he could imagine it perfectly. Carrying a weight, a weariness he had never felt before, he climbed the slope again, with difficulty, and continued his walk to school.

That day, at lunch, upon arriving at the front entrance of City Hall, he stopped, surprised, and asked himself: what am I doing here?

Once home, as they ate lunch, served by the old lady, he told his parents what had happened. The Master of the house shrugged his shoulders, and the Mistress said: "Finally, our room will be free."

That afternoon, Fenix locked himself in his room and didn't go back to school. Lying in bed, shivering under a blanket, so anxious he couldn't cry, without even realizing that he was anxious, for the first time, he asked himself questions about the future. He tried to imagine what life would be like without Captain Vorosoff, who had been a substitute father to him, maybe more loved than the one he had, who meticulously got ready in front of the mirror before leaving and becoming a ghost.

According to his father, the leftover wood that had been saved from his artisanal factory was what was used to build a coffin for Vorosoff. Without eulogies, without much ceremony at all, but in a silence resembling the extension of the silence of death, they buried him in the central square, in his uniform, with his medals and the Luger, so he could make Saint Peter open the gates to him, or battle with Satan, under the serene, tender gaze of the Virgin up on her pillar, alongside other Russian officers who were already resting in the same place. On the side of the city square, a monument to the fallen heroes of the war was built, a kind of obelisk with the hammer and sickle engraved. Years later, when Fenix would return to his small native city, he would realize that they had exhumed the officers' bodies, without being able to identify them with certainty. For Fenix, who would walk around the square and every now and then stop in front of the grass, Vorosoff would still be there in a grave that became anonymous; just another unknown soldier. The only thing left of him, if anyone had kept it, would have been the telegram that his family would have received announcing his heroic death in combat for the glory of the Soviet Union, the Proletarians of the World and Comrade Stalin.

Remembering him fondly every now and again, Fenix would ask himself if Captain Vorosoff was human. There was no doubt in his mind. Without knowing exactly what the word "human" meant, Fenix knew that (in addition to his deep loving relationship with Judit), albeit for only a brief lapse of time, the embraces, the protection, the affection of Captain Vorosoff, had left a mark on him forever; no less than Judit, he had taught him to embrace, to understand, to listen, to protect his children rather than lashing out and slapping them, to let them enter into the mirror that he almost never looked at himself in.

Of course, Fenix didn't deceive himself; he saw Vorosoff for what he really was. He knew perfectly well that the medals that he boasted about hadn't been won for pilgrimages to the Calvary or the Holy Land, but for Germans crucified mercilessly, without confession, without blessings, with or without their hands up. In any case, without suffering shell shock, the Captain had a very clear idea of things, whether he was right or not; in addition to the invasion of a territory, of the global triumph of communism, he had other, more simple causes, tender ones, one might say, less ambitious. Every week, Captain Vorosoff would show him the black and white pictures of his family, talk to him about his five children, two of whom were studying to become engineers and would become part of the great *intelligentsia* of Russia or the Soviet Union, model of justice and well-being, that sooner or later, all of humanity would follow. He would lament that one of them didn't want to study, out of laziness or foolishness, but his two daughters did, though it was toward a lesser career: medicine. With deep sighs, sometimes shedding a tear or two, he would tell him that he missed them very much, just like his wife, whom he loved both as the mother of his children and as a lover, whose absence he would compensate for (here he would wink) with visits to the bar. Not many, no, not at all; he had responsibilities to attend to and would only do it when it became unbearable. He would go reluctantly, he would say, undoubtedly propelled by a demon inside him that he didn't believe in, and always returned feeling guilty.

Vorosoff's body never returned to the palace for them to bid farewell; such a ceremony had likely taken place somewhere else. The day after his death, with an officer, only his assistant appeared to look for the papers that probably identified Vorosoff. Maybe a few others, those called "secret" or "compromising." For two hours, they opened and closed drawers, doors, even lifted the bottle of vodka a few times to see if there was something underneath, and the bottle would land on the table again, a little lighter each time, like an airplane that had discharged its bombs. Fenix's father listened through the sliding door and, when they left, heard the officer say:

"We'll have to come back for all his belongings, to send them to his family."

"Yes, of course, to his family. But let's go now, lieutenant, they've been waiting for us for a while."

—⁓ 22.

❧——**TWO WEEKS LATER**, the commander who replaced Vorosoff, whom Fenix didn't know (it was hard for him to imagine that there could be another commander, but he was aware of his existence because of the effects he caused), gave the order to pack their bags, put the trucks into gear, line up the tanks and, in all the excitement, the shouting, and the vodka that flowed, return home, to Russia. Or perhaps it was nothing more than the joy of moving at all, after almost a year of immobility.

However, this wasn't the only command. The dust that the army's march had lifted hadn't yet settled when the detachment that the new commander had left—it wasn't known what for, whether it was in order to watch their backs or not to leave the little city unprotected—without knowing from what or whom, or perhaps they would soon see—organized one more cleansing operation.

For the last time in the history of the town, as though it were a resurrection, the news herald reappeared, and the drummer with his drum. He wasn't wearing his strange flamboyant uniform, it's true, but with a soldier holding a machine gun standing beside him, he certainly drew attention. At every corner the drum rolled, but without the enthusiasm of before; the neighbours ran and, this time, only speaking Slovak, which sounded a little strange, the herald announced: "To anyone who has housed any brave member of the Red Army of any rank: if the aforementioned member has left behind any personal effects or any objects belonging to the Red Army that do not belong to the owner of the property, an object that is foreign and not their property and that the aforementioned brave soldier would have brought with him and left behind or abandoned after his departure, who answers to a superior commander, in the next twenty-four hours, the owner of the property must report the object to the relevant military authorities, that is to say, military officers who will remain for a few days to collect the aforementioned objects. In addition to collecting the reported objects, within three days, there will be an inspection and anyone having defaulted on or hindered this operation, the object then being considered stolen, will be punished with imprisonment and condemned to years of prison directly proportional to the value of the object they have attempted to hide."

Even without cause, everyone feared being accused of theft. Since there was practically no house where something wasn't left behind, scraps in most cases (a canteen, a torn military jacket, ammunition belts for machine guns, empty bottles of vodka), many hounded the drummer to ask him where they should report to. The drummer answered that he didn't know exactly, that it would be in some part of the city, that they should ask the soldier who was with him, who in turn simply shrugged. To free themselves of any potential sentence, most of the objects were left in front of City Hall to rot under the rain, if they weren't rotten already.

These random events of life, in this case of war, are what are sometimes called miracles. Entering into someone's home to capture and shoot them, and that someone, at the exact same moment, leaving through the back door, where they had forgotten to station a guard. Or, despite the mistrust of those who know human malice through confessions (the police, the military, priests ...), believing that a person is who they say they are, or in reality seeing nothing more than who they "should" be. Although they suspected him, as evidenced by the quarantine he was kept in, something similar happened with Fenix's father.

On the evening of the announcement, when Fenix came home from school, before going into his bedroom, to evade the old lady's kisses, he took the path through the living room, where, in front of a coffee table, on a sofa, he found his mother and father, sitting close together like two lovers, one might say, if it weren't for Fenix noticing the pitcher that Vorosoff had poured the lighter stones out of. Out of surprise, Fenix had forgotten to greet them and, silent, he stood in front of them, staring at the pitcher.

"What's the matter? Cat got your tongue? Is this how I raised you? Get out of here, leave us alone, we need to talk," his sweet mother barked.

His mother's beatings, wounds that were thankfully non-permanent, made him form a shield that he would put on every time he would feel attacked, and he began using it that very night. He left his schoolbag in his bedroom without opening it, with the idea that not doing his homework was a form of vengeance against his mother who mistreated him, and his father who didn't defend him, motives that were more than sufficient to justify not wanting to do it.

Since he didn't want to see his parents, instead of doing it in the dining room, he decided to go back to eating in the kitchen, and there he went, with his shield ready. Just as the old woman was about to hug and welcome him, to avoid the slobbery kisses that would come next, he stopped her in her tracks.

"Leave me alone, don't touch me ... please," he said, and he took a seat at the table.

The woman, the sweet woman who wasn't personally to blame for the disgust she inspired in him, served him dinner in silence. Who knows whether Fenix noticed her moist eyes and, before they rolled down her face, the tears that she wiped with her apron? Maybe in his old age, remembering the woman, he would feel a certain discomfort without knowing why.

When, in the morning, he got up to go to school, he had the feeling that the space in the palace, as though there hadn't already been enough, had widened, and he could breathe a little better. What had disappeared, in fact, were his parents. In addition to the woman, who served him breakfast in the dining room, there he found his grandfather, who informed him that his parents needed to take an urgent trip and that they would be gone for two or three days, depending.

"Depending on what, grandpa?"

A shudder came over the grandfather, who without realizing it looked toward the bedroom in which Vorosoff had lived.

"Well, I don't know ... no, no, I don't know ..." His voice was the echo of his shuddering. A pause, then: "Business, maybe. Yes, business. But don't worry; while they're gone, I'll take care of you. That's why I'm here."

Whether because of his age, or simply his nature, since Fenix had come into the world, this is how he knew him, the grandfather's character had always been a little sullen. This included his relationship with his daughter, which would never stop being tense. And since the Mistress was the most powerful of all her sisters, her kitchen was better supplied, had a beautiful living room with ceramic stove for the winter days, the grandfather would visit the palace but, apart from a few affectionate taps on the head, or making little comments to him, he had never really gotten to know Fenix, who, to tell the truth, because he had Judit, never concerned himself with getting to know his grandfather very well either. However, without being able to express it with words, Fenix's body perceived that, in addition to the grandfather's shuddering, something more was happening in his soul. It was enough to hear the tone of his voice, especially when he asked:

"Do you want me to take you to school? I have the horse and carriage here."

Fenix looked at him, puzzled. He thanked him for his offer; however:

"Thank you, grandfather, but I prefer to go alone."

The grandfather reacted as though he had been punched. The word "prefer" had been devastating. His grey eyes, already watery, became even wetter. Thank goodness, before finishing his coffee, with his mug raised as he took his last sip, Fenix saw his eyes and intuited what was happening.

"It's not because of you, grandfather. It's just like with my cousins. They don't let me think."

A sigh of relief from the grandfather, and:

"Think? About what? Some philosophical problem?"

Fenix didn't know what the word *philosophical* meant (he was almost certain that his grandfather didn't either; he must have heard it from some politician ... "*our philosophy* ..."), but, since he was indeed the Mistress's father and she his daughter, Fenix could sense a light teasing tone in the questions. And so, instead of answering the truth that didn't stop weighing on him and saddening him: "It's just that Judit comes with me, and we chat about our business, and we don't like being interrupted," he said, then got up, took his school bag and added:

"Thank you, ma'am. See you at dinner."

"What?" said his grandfather and the woman, almost in unison. "You're not coming back for lunch?"

"No, I'm going to stay at school with the children who get a glass of milk and some bread. See you later."

Seconds after the grandfather's questions, in Captain Vorosoff's absence, he decided to go to the cemetery to visit Judit. How many times did he imagine her as the Sleeping Beauty, and himself as the Prince! And he knew that all that was needed was a kiss.

However, it didn't happen this way. He had gone but found her bed covered in earth, a cloak he had forgotten existed. And on top of this cloak, another, a little more pleasant, layer of yellow and red leaves, that even though they were part of the sadness of autumn, could also mean more warmth and protection for her. Even from the rain, the first drops of which began to fall as Fenix left the cemetery.

His parents would take almost a month to reappear. During that time, the detachment that had remained after the army's departure departed in turn. Once and for all, the little city remained in the hands of the civilian authorities. Whether the NKVD left some secret agent in an even more secret office somewhere, no one could be sure. The days were also getting shorter. Fenix, his cousins and his friends stopped playing ball in the street earlier and earlier. The leaves ended up falling from the trees. The cold days multiplied, during which they had to light the stove in the living room and the grandfather, at night, after dinner, would take his place in his armchair with a glass of wine, and between the *pap pap*s from his pipe, as though they were detaching from the clouds of smoke, the old songs emerged again, though much quieter. Autumn had clearly settled in and would soon give way to winter. Fenix doesn't remember precisely, although his grandfather and the old lady were already talking about the Day of the Dead and the need to prepare candles.

Only miracles occur in an instant, which is why they are miracles. What is more, life is a process, very often a painful one, that takes our time, so much so that it devours life itself. Fenix and his grandfather never ignored each other, but they didn't give each other much acknowledgement or affection, either. Sometimes, in the middle of the summer, or very close to the harvest, Fenix would go with him to the Calvary to inspect the state of the vineyard, and of the grapes that his grandfather would feel as gently as he would an intimate body part, like a woman's breast. If they were ripe, he would cut a beautiful bunch of muscatel grapes so that Fenix could fill his belly. However, what would have helped them bond even more would be accompanying his grandfather on his excursions to the surrounding areas to distribute the wine, his mother, in one of the rare manifestations of her attention, had forbidden it, since, because he was always a little drunk, the carriage seemed to be driven by the horse.

Maybe that wasn't the case; maybe it was nothing more than a way of exacting revenge for something that had happened in the past, and more than to protect Fenix, she was denying her father the joy of being with his grandson. And so, during his parents' absence, on weekends, very early in the morning, the grandfather, after making sure that he was properly bundled up, would extend his hand out to Fenix to help him climb up into the carriage, usually already stocked up. If it wasn't, they would pass by the winery to fill the demijohns, a real adventure during which, in the darkness, among the barrels, the casks, the different levels, he would discover the hideouts of ogres, gnomes, labyrinths of dwarves—a little immature for him, in truth, since he had already grown too old for these fairy tales that emerged from the pages of the books that Judit had read to him, or from the stories that she told, but, regardless, these were a confirmation of their legendary existence. He never discovered Ali Baba's cave and would continue searching for it all his life, in vain.

The pleasure of adventure continued through narrow paths between the half-bare trees with their branches of silver or gold, as they climbed and descended the slopes and valleys; an adventure more imagined than real, without being surprised (apart from now that he remembers it) by the discovery of taverns in tiny villages, or the more mysterious ones, isolated in the middle of forests or at the intersections of paths. And he must confess that, just like the grandfather, two or three times he put his trust in the horse while, half-asleep, he would put his arms around his grandfather, who was also leaning on him.

Since there had been a precedent, this absence of Fenix's parents served to revive the embers, reaffirm the ties already established and create new ones. So much so, that, to the best of his memory, two or three times his grandfather went to meet him as he left school and brought him home, holding his hand.

Unfortunately, the grandfather was so insistent in his need to reaffirm these bonds that he didn't realize that Fenix had grown and, at his age, now a young man, it would embarrass him a little to be holding hands (although it is common to see tender old couples doing it, they actually do so to lean on each other so that they won't fall). If he had been a woman, if it had been Judit ... but she was resting.

And so, although a miracle occurred, it wasn't a full nor a

complete one. Maybe it was too late, or maybe it was interrupted by the return of his parents who were now stuck together like Siamese twins, or two lovebirds, who had just discovered that they would love each other eternally, or even accomplices working toward the ambitious adventure that would change Fenix's life and destiny.

Fenix's father was a man of the Communist Party, and as a result, trustworthy, although in past circumstances they had not trusted him (they had lifted the quarantine and now, apparently, saw in him the man that he should be instead of the one who was likely to escape through the back door, without thinking of what he would do through another, right in front of them). With the belongings that Vorosoff had left behind, his father was playing with fire and he knew it. Although it is true that the Inquisition no longer existed, and pyres weren't being made to burn the sinners, there was something similar in Siberia, where the Soviet Union was also being built, and where quite a lot of labour was required. This Fenix's father knew as well. And he knew something more, not through wisdom, but because it had been whispered to him in exchange for a few dinars: whatever he did, as much trust as they seemed to have in him, sooner or later he would be sent off to run an artisanal factory in Siberia. He had no other recourse left but to be brave and have the ingenuity—this he deserves credit for—to leave through the big door, the one that they weren't monitoring.

⟿ 23.

FENIX'S FATHER, AS a first step to balance things, took charge of the rest of the stones that, most likely, no one would reclaim. Selling them wasn't the booming business that it had been a year earlier. In the filthy sphere of business, a more unfair competitor always emerges. However, they had some value and were easily portable, like a currency of exchange, very useful for the trip that his parents had undertaken without telling him where they were going, and that was the most elegant and cunning way of ignoring the military order. *After me, the flood.* If by the time they returned, Vorosoff's treasure had been discovered and taken, they would see. It was a bit of an ostrich tactic; they may not necessarily be able to evade responsibilities, but it didn't hurt to try.

Apart from the many mysteries surrounding whether one stays alive in a war or dies in it, there are others, not related to life, but rather to riches: how is it that Vorosoff's things stayed in the bedroom that he had occupied in the palace? The speculations could be many. The helper with the folder didn't dare come back to look for them because a sub-officer wouldn't be able to justify objects of such value being in his saddlebag. The lieutenant may have received an order diverting him from the proper course of return to collect the things. He would have searched for the opportunity to find a shortcut but it wouldn't have presented itself and, greedy, he wouldn't have wanted to share the secret of Ali Baba's treasure with a superior who would have facilitated his task, for the price of sharing the treasure. Or it was simply forgotten, or maybe a bureaucratic oversight on the part of the military that, upon seeing Vorosoff's name written on the list of heroes and crossed out on the list of troops, assumed that everything that he had left behind had been crossed out as well. And the treasure, with the exception of the lighter stones, remained there.

The slave owner, with tears in his eyes after reading *Uncle Tom's Cabin*, feels good about himself for providing work for his slaves, and proud for only beating them a little. For Fenix, when his father conducted business with his inner self regarding Vorosoff's things and spoke of it explicitly out loud, the matter was no different from the slave master's reasoning.

The objects that Vorosoff had collected from other palaces in other countries were bought by his father for the price of the boards used to build the coffin they had buried him in, to which he added other boards of other coffins and the wood used for the bridge. From the little stones (of which there were none left, not even one for his own lighter), to the samovar that ended up being full of silver, crystals, vases, a porcelain tea set from China, boxes full of watches and jewellery, everything slowly disappeared, until finishing with the huge rug cut into smaller ones and fixed by a seamstress to be, like everything else, sold to rich peasants with bourgeois aspirations, to the professionals of the small city and, among the few Jews that returned, to one or two jewellers who, by burying them, had saved their treasures from the greed of the two armies, and upon digging them up, resumed their trade, advertising with a poster over the ruins: "We Buy Gold." Like in a fairy tale, all the objects were transforming into green papers that Fenix saw being counted in the living room (by the two lovebirds, sitting close together) and that according to what he would discover later, was the lifeblood of the twentieth century, that nurtured joy, triumph, luxury cemeteries and more wars, as though the one that had just passed hadn't been enough. For the moment, it was the mother who was in charge of accumulating them to pay for the passport that, on a secret mission, would allow them to leave through the big door.

Who knows, another mystery? A noble gesture from his father that made them neglect to monitor the big door? What is certain is that, because of the dangers implied in possessing guns, they didn't know what on earth to do with the box of revolvers and the armchair upholstered with velvet that they couldn't sell. The Comrades from the Party would receive them with satisfaction, especially the armchair. They drew up an agreement and thanked them for their honesty.

⇌ 24.

THE DAYS PASSED, and, that autumn, the Day of the Dead finally came. Candles were lit and placed on the graves. The cemetery populated with the living and the dead, in dialogue. The dead complaining without moving from their beds. The living, swearing that they would do for them now what they had never done when they were on Earth (hold masses, for example).

It was one of Fenix's last visits until he would come back thirty or forty years later. He had gone with his cousins, uncles and aunts, his grandfather and his mother. It was a pleasant evening, a kind of little summer—Fenix doesn't remember what it is called there, summer of Saint John or Saint Martin. The family was large: the grandmother, the great-grandparents and great-great-grandparents, and a few uncles were there: the prayers, the reunions, the discussions with the dead, the old quarrels, the reproaches, were re-emerging. The conversations, the attempts at reconciliation, once more, were prolonged and threatened to become eternal.

Was Fenix bored? Probably. He had already prayed many

times to the uncle who had died of tuberculosis—if the medication had existed he would still be alive, how intelligent he was, really promising; someone else who had died in the First World War, very nice, everyone remembered him, a little bit of a boozer, though ... Fenix was parched and hungry. He had wandered off from his cousins and was walking around the illuminated streets, between people kneeling and mumbling prayers, silent silhouettes of the living, shadows of the dead, modest graves with few flowers and some candles, others, with sculptures of angels, marble headstones and enough candles to light a theatre, that marked social differences without him, at this moment, being in a state to theorize on class struggles in cemeteries.

But this grave, dark in the darkness, an even darker well, with the earth sunk in by gravity that couldn't stop nor support the rotting casket, without a headstone, barely even a wooden cross, crooked, about to fall, with a blurry name that he couldn't manage to read in the shadows, was familiar to him. Could it be ...?

Among so many graves, he wanted to be sure. From a nearby burial mound on which some candles were wilting, he took one. Burning his fingers, he brought the flame to the cross without touching it; leaning in, he spelled out the letters one by one by the light of the candle, revealing the name. He put them all together: "Horvath Family." Had he forgotten her? No, he knew that Judit, his Sleeping Beauty, was there waiting for him. However, when he had come a month or two ago, it didn't go the way he had dreamed it; his Sleeping Beauty hadn't been there waiting to be kissed by her prince. Moreover, the earth had sunk and it was as though she had distanced herself even further; from him, from this world.

He left the candle at the edge of the sunken soil and from

which emanated a moist gentle breeze with a faint smell of mould, somewhat sweet. Unsettled, surprised, on the verge of tears, he gathered more candles in a quick scramble, along with some of the flowers, and began placing them on the Horvath grave. When he knelt to pray for Judit's eternal rest, tears fell down his cheeks. A strange, frozen breeze blew in from nowhere, a temptation to dive underneath the flowers and candles that were slowly going out and slipping into the dark well.

A strange kind of pain inside, down to his bones; a crack, maybe of growth: without being consciously aware of it, he knew then that it was useless to live as he had been living, waiting, at every moment, at every instant, to find her sleeping, believing that he could wake her with a kiss, that she would walk in through the door, that she would lift him up in the air, and then ... and then, in front of the fire ... with a little train going *choo choo* ... heading toward ...

When his mother saw him appear, she thought she had seen a ghost. But it was no more than a moment in the life of her son, the moment when he abandoned his childhood skin and began to grow one that was tougher, more resistant. To Fenix's question about what had happened to Judit's grave, his mother said that the family, as far as she knew, had no more relatives left in the city, and no one knew if there were any distant ones somewhere else. So what about if we decorate it ourselves? No way, let the dead care for their dead, we don't have the time ... or the money ... the Germans took the machines from our factory ... the Russians the wood ... and now that we're thinking of emig ...

"But she's sad, and alone."

"Not at all, her entire family is with her. Let's not speak of this anymore."

Yes, out of love, to distract him, to bring him away from

there, or so as not to lose him now that they were about to head home, his mother took his hand. Taking advantage of being in a sacred place, Fenix continued to insist. It's true that he didn't get slapped, but this time, not from growth but from the brutal clasp of her hand, the bones in his fingers cracked. And in case it wasn't clear, a vigorous violent shake made him understand that the discussion was over.

⤳ 25.

☞—**IT'S NOT THAT** he wasn't able to do it alone, but he needed an accomplice to mitigate the possible consequences of his idea, which today would be called a plan or project. The day after the visit to the cemetery, at school, like someone proposing a great adventure that entailed a mysterious and unknown danger, but nothing too difficult, he managed to convince one of his cousins, who also was his playmate, a kind of little brother that Fenix never had and who, in spite of being the same age as Fenix, because of his size inspired fear. Maybe because his mother never stopped showing a certain dislike toward him due to being a poor parent, so that his arguments could be more convincing, in addition to the words "courage" and "bravery," Fenix emphasized that "we will make a lot of money."

In the afternoon, after school, they casually made the trip to the entrance of the cemetery. They slipped discreetly through the open gate like two grave robbers. There was no need: the drunk guard that only ever got up to greet the dead (it was said that the dead needed to wake him for him to greet them) was sleeping, as usual.

But they needed to give a certain tone, touch or flavour to

the undertaking, of a business venture or the conquest of the West. Crawling between the graves, stopping to kneel or crouch in front of each, they collected the leftover candles, melted wax mixed with holy earth, autumn leaves, withered flower petals, some larger candles that had been blown out by the wind or the neglect of one of the deceased's loved ones, and filled their backpacks.

They returned home. Fenix would have preferred to stay quiet, but his aunt, worried about his cousin's tardiness, was already there and the interrogation began, almost with the same intensity as if it were the police. They had forgotten to come up with a good excuse, if there could possibly have been one, and his cousin confessed. When they showed the leftover candles, horror and dismay. Fenix's calm explanations of their reason, "to make and sell candles," was considered a sacrilege by the aunt who, with a resounding slap, removed his cousin from the business.

Fenix, for the first time in his life, was spared his mother's inquisitorial punishment of spending hours kneeling on corn, by his father, the atheistic communist enlightened by the Age of Enlightenment, a profound believer in progress. Even if in this moment, his small fortune was due to intensive bartering of objects left behind by others, he had faith that in the near future, thanks to his talent, with more modern machines to make artisanal objects, he would launder his capital and in so doing triple its value without forgetting the proletariat, modern slaves. In another world, obviously.

Not only did he defend Fenix ("Ha! Sacrilege, an idea from the Middle Ages, ridiculous ... This is the Twentieth Century, diesel motors are a reality ... and who knows what's yet to come ...") but, leading the charge of modern pedagogy, he commended him for his initiative, motivation and creativity.

Like father, like son: he didn't show any less talent and forward-thinking spirit than his father. He discovered, forty years before its time, a technique that would save the world: applied recycling. There is no doubt that in the absence of an instruction or D.I.Y. manual for candle recycling, a special chapter for candles stolen from the graves of the dead, he showed considerable precociousness and skill. Without his cousin, as one hundred percent stockholder, with a feverish activity that his mother called "infernal" with a revolted look on her face, in the courtyard, humming a tune, in an old pot on top of a fire that he had lit himself, he melted the candles and filtered the wax to clean it of impurities and, in cardboard moulds, holding the wick until the wax hardened, he made fifteen candles—perhaps not of impeccable quality, but perfectly usable.

And one additional one that, in an act of generosity, an attempt at winning her favour, he wanted to give to his mother so that she could put it on her nightstand; generosity that his mother, in addition to another disgusted face, instead of "Oh, what a nice gift, thank you" (his mother, as we have seen, knew absolutely nothing of pedagogical guidelines to build self-esteem), not only gave him a slap that Fenix, now an expert, managed to evade, but, while making little horns, howled: "*Vade retro Satanas!*"

He put it on his own nightstand. The others, he kept in the basement to sell next year, when share prices would increase during the season of the dead.

The city residents noticed what he had done. There was no shortage of admiration and comments: "Crafty, that kid, eh?" "Yes, he sure has initiative!" "Too bad it's a little macabre ..." "Even Dracula wouldn't have thought of it." There was even one person who wanted to buy one or two candles as a souvenir of "such a nice little Dracula" and, incidentally, asked his father, or his mortified mother, how much they cost. His father, on the other hand, was very content. Although he disliked merchants, he was still proud of his son's commercial skills, as well as his techniques that, in the ultramodern world that awaited them, whatever happened (he himself was an example), would at least allow him to live a comfortable life, in case he didn't have the brains to be a doctor or engineer or scientist. Fenix, for his part, concluded that, precisely, to be a doctor or an engineer or a great scientist, one needed a certain dose of stupidity or blindness. Obviously, he may have been speaking out of resentment.

—⁊ 26.

&—HOWEVER, THE FOLLOWING year, the Day of the Dead, in the little city, would never come. The factory had disappeared and his father's activities had reached their limit. The goods, the basis of his trade and metamorphosis, had become scarce, or had stopped existing altogether. The anonymous reports, the increasingly firm control of the communist patriots who began to suspect that the comrade whom they saw as he "should be," wasn't so, threatened to bring him to jail for a third time. Once he realized the threat of leading an artisanal factory in Siberia, he self-imposed what during decades would be called (even if they went by train or boat) "the flight to freedom." Freedom, a golden cage without bars, from which there is no return nor escape.

They would go, but where? They told Fenix it was on vacation, a long vacation, very long. During a few weeks, there was unusual movement, comings and goings of neighbours, strange visits, the selling of paintings, of china, of silverware, of furniture, even the grandfather's armchair; everything converted into gold coins and, preferably, as Fenix remembers it, once more into bills of green paper. The interminable whispers between his parents, the secretive atmosphere, with a little fear but full of optimism, suggested something more than a long vacation; it seemed more like it was going to be eternal in some place similar to Paradise with its golden fruits.

A few weeks before leaving, at night time, his father, as though he were coming to share a revelation, in secret, arrived with a taste of the marvellous world they were going to: a strange fruit wrapped in white tissue paper and a box, maybe the last of those he sold as contraband. He put it on the table, under his nostrils. The fragrance, *sniff,* intoxicated him. With care, he unwrapped it and, instead of an apple, appeared the yellow surface of a fruit he had never seen and that, they told him, was called an "orange." *Sniff,* he looked at his parents, who were smiling. "Can you eat it?" he asked them, and they nodded. He lifted it, studied it and bit into it; his mouth filled with a bitter taste: he spat. His parents burst out laughing; silly, you don't eat the peel but what's inside, like with nuts. Plaff, Fenix slammed it onto the table. Who knows how far the orange had travelled before arriving here; a little past its prime, almost rotten, it burst. Fenix began to cry.

His father, with a tenderness unbecoming of him, slipping into a conceited tone, consoled him:

"Don't worry, where we're going, a real Paradise, where the apple of discord isn't known; they only eat the oranges of harmony, of peace and love. And believe us: there are tons."

And on the table, he pushed the box in front of him.

"Take it, so that it gives you an idea of this place. This box comes from there; it's a chest that contains real treasure."

It was a flat rectangular box: a real taste of the marvellous world out there. It was Fenix's first contact with what are now called elements of globalization. On the wider part of the box, the drawing of the contents of its compartments was printed;

Fenix didn't recognize any part of it. In the upper left part it read in big letters: "*U.S.A. Army*," and other words, smaller, that no one could understand. Parts of the box were perforated with small holes and, with the legend *pull* or *push*, there were little arrows that pointed toward different parts, but that didn't seem to lead anywhere. Not knowing the meaning of the arrows, not understanding the words, Fenix, naturally, asked:

"How do I open it?"

His father didn't know; he sighed and said:

"I must admit that I'm not sure. We're not properly educated nor prepared. Many hardships await us. Let me have a look."

God only knows the mysteries of human meanderings; whether it was because he didn't trust his father for some completely unknown reason (had he kept part of this treasure for himself, or would his mother have gotten her hands on it?); because he wanted to challenge him and show that he was just as capable than him, if not more so; or just on a whim, nothing more, without saying "No" and without knowing a thing about the legend of the Gordian knot nor the method used by Alexander to undo it; with his index finger he decided to enlarge one of the holes, and when he put it in, the surface that linked it with the other holes broke, gave in with astonishing ease, and Fenix was able to slip his finger under the cover to then pull up the entire surface that, in different compartments, allowed them to discover its marvellous contents: a little bar of chocolate, some gum, bouillon cubes, packets of coffee, tea and sugar, a little plastic spoon, a mini box full of cigarettes and matches, a pack of salted peanuts. Between the three of them, they ate everything. His parents smoked the cigarettes, which they found marvellous, perfumed, fragrant, with a Virginia flavour, much praised and never tried before; and Fenix, after eating the chocolate, which because of its poor quality he was sure that Judit wouldn't have liked it, undertook the task of eating the mint-flavoured gum.

It's late; to bed. No, there was no way he would ever finish eating the gum. In any case, it had already lost its flavour; he spat it out. Before leaving the table, Fenix snatched the tissue paper and took it with him. In his pyjamas, sitting on the edge of his bed, he smoothed the paper on his pillow: a stamp appeared, a kind of map, underneath, along the circumference, he spelled out: *An-da-lu-cí-a. Sp-a-in.* He left the paper on the nightstand, next to the candle and a book of stories by the Brothers Grimm, full of magic and miracles, that Judit used to read to him and now, still with a bit of difficulty, he read to himself. He lay down, asking himself when they would leave to go to *Andalucía, Spain, Andalucía, Spa* ...

They would leave very soon, but Fenix would never get to Andalucia.

—⁓ 27.

❧——**CLASSES HAD ENDED** and there were only a few days left before their departure but, because of the wait, in a practically empty, hollow, house, they were indecisive, uncertain to the limit of fears impossible to define. They were wondering: would the big door be closed?

Under the summer sun there were walks that seemed like an anticipation of the promised vacation. Walks along the riverbank and through the centre of the little city. For worse or for worse, in addition to the bakery that had increased its selection and notably improved its ice cream, some other businesses had now reopened and they were removing the rubble from one of the church towers that had been brought down by a cannon shot or a bomb. The other tower, the bell tower, had remained intact. In the little square, after taking a few walks around, his mother and an aunt were sitting on a bench, chatting. Without a friend with whom to play, Fenix was bored. He crossed the street, approached the church; it was as natural as putting himself in a kind of cell underneath the bell tower and from the punctured ceiling of which hung different sized ropes. He grabbed the thickest one and tried to swing, but it didn't even move. He tried another thinner one and, surprise, ding, ding again, he got excited and, ding ding ding. A total success: three minutes later, in addition to his mother, people arrived asking who had died. Some laughed, others grumbled. The threat he received and the slaps he evaded aren't worth discussing. And in an era when the life or death of someone, apart from the heirs and morticians rubbing their hands together, piqued interest in others and they would even lament it as an absence, an eternal emptiness, perhaps not that either.

The day of their departure came. The relatives, with hugs and promises, had already said goodbye and were waiting for the last classic salutations: waving goodbye. Fed up with waiting, most of the relatives said goodbye once more and went home. The tenant who had rented the house, with a smile on his face, an heir thinking that the owners would never return from where they were going, watched the car that was waiting, with the mother sitting in the back seat. The grandfather would have needed to leave with the old horse and carriage, to arrive on time to the station, hug them, perhaps for the last time, and watch as the train vanished in the distance. But he hadn't done it, Fenix had disappeared, and now the grandfather was walking around calling him, shouting his name. His father, now tired of searching for him, was discussing with the conductor the possibility of going to Prague if they missed the local train in order not to miss the International.

But they didn't miss it. Running, sweating, red, frantic, as though he had committed a crime, Fenix appeared. The threats or reproaches were useless, although he did end up provoking them. The moment he arrived, he ran inside without his father's shouting being able to stop him, and, a few endless minutes later, came out with the book of stories and the locomotive from the electric train whose rediscovery, after his parents had emptied

Vorosoff's bedroom, had shaken his soul quite significantly: the infinite joy at having found what, through the most beautiful tunnel imaginable, had brought him to Heaven on earth, the Celestial Pillow; the relief and the cleansing of guilt for having "sold" it for an object there was nothing sacred about (quite the opposite); the disillusionment, the disappointment in Vorosoff for having lied to him and not having sent the train to his sons and, with his inner child, having spent his time playing with the train (he couldn't bring himself to give him the benefit of the doubt; maybe he had forgotten to send it, or had wanted to bring it personally as a surprise for his children).

Irresponsible, inconsiderate, stupid, where did you go? And the locomotive, at your age, if we miss the train, I'll ...

But they didn't miss it. Once on board, in the first-class cabin, with Fenix sitting on the side of the window, he felt the shake and heard the first choo-choos of the big locomotive as it departed on its way to Prague.

On his feet, with his nose stuck to the window, and the locomotive in his hand, he watched as the train, accelerating and tracing a curve, distanced itself; the Calvary, the church, the city, the river, were shrinking, and disappeared all at once when, with the accelerated choo-choos, the train entered the tunnel and the cabin went dark.

His grandfather didn't get there in time to hug them. On foot on the platform, he watched as the train distanced itself, and stayed there, waving his hand, until the shadow of the tunnel devoured the last wagon.

In the darkness, he hugged his locomotive with such force that it hurt his arm. With tears in his eyes, Fenix thought with joy of the fifteen candles that adorned the Horvath family grave and would illuminate the bedroom where Judit slept, waiting for him to give her the kiss that would awaken her.

In the darkness of the cabin, pairs of eyes appeared, and stared at him: the dead soldier in the courtyard, the fool of the hill, the captain; hundreds of eyes, among which Judit's golden ones threatened to become lost. In the cabin or in his mind?

It was useless for him to cover his eyes.

About the Author

PABLO URBANYI was born in Hungary in 1939. At the age of eight, he emigrated to Argentina, where he grew up, was educated, and wrote and published his first two books, a collection of short stories and a novel. From 1975 to 1977, the year he emigrated to Canada, he worked as an editor for the cultural supplement of the newspaper "La Opinión" in Buenos Aires. In Canada he continued writing. He published *Sunset* (1997), *Silver* (1995) (finalist for the Argentine Planeta award), and *El zoológico de Dios* (2006), all translated into Hungarian, French and English. His writing is characterized by critical humour, and a subtle and profound irony. In addition to being a Planeta finalist, he has received other awards and mentions: he was the winner of the 2004 Somos la Expresión Literaria Award, Latin American Achievement Awards, Toronto. His native city, Ipolyság in Hungary, named him Honorary Citizen for his literary achievements. He has given lectures, seminars, and readings in Germany, Spain, and France, and published five more books. He is a member of PEN International.

About the Translator

NATALIA HERO is a writer and literary translator based in Montreal, Quebec. She holds a B.A. in English and Spanish literature from Concordia University and an M.A. in literary translation from the University of Ottawa. She translates works from French and Spanish into English and is the author of the novella *Hum* (Metatron Press, 2018).

Printed in August 2020
by Gauvin Press,
Gatineau, Québec